THE MAN WITH THE CAMERA EYES

Investigative lawyer Langton has solved many bizarre cases with the help of his friend Peter Crewe, who possesses such an extraordinary photographic memory that he never forgets a face. Here Langton relates twelve stories featuring audacious jewel robberies, scientific geniuses gone mad and bad, and cold-blooded murder served up via amusement park rides, craftily concealed explosives, and hot air balloons. In each, the Man with the Camera Eyes provides the observations and deductions that are crucial to the solution of the mystery — often risking his own life in the process . . .

Books by Victor Rousseau
in the Linford Mystery Library:

THE WHITE LILY MURDER

VICTOR ROUSSEAU

THE MAN
WITH THE
CAMERA EYES

Complete and Unabridged

LINFORD
Leicester

First published in Great Britain

First Linford Edition
published 2016

A catalogue record for this book is available
from the British Library.

ISBN 978–1–4448–2953–2

Published by
F. A. Thorpe (Publishing)
Anstey, Leicestershire

Set by Words & Graphics Ltd.
Anstey, Leicestershire
Printed and bound in Great Britain by
T. J. International Ltd., Padstow, Cornwall

This book is printed on acid-free paper

1

The Box of Borneos

It was a rough passage, and though we were already halfway between New York and Tilbury, our destination, few of the passengers had found their sea legs. I sat on the captain's right; upon his left was a pleasant, florid, gray-haired man, rather slow of speech, who was introduced to me as Mr. Peter Crewe.

'Do you find that this Atlantic breeze agrees with you better than the air of Plainfield, New Jersey, Mr. Langton?' asked Mr. Crewe politely.

'It certainly does,' I answered. 'But may I ask you how on earth you know that I'm a resident of Plainfield, New Jersey? To the best of my belief I haven't told anyone; in fact, as a lawyer, I'm naturally secretive about such matters.'

'I only know,' replied Crewe, 'because on two occasions I've seen you hurrying

1

to the boat from the New Jersey terminal at nine o'clock in the morning. You carried a newspaper and a suitcase, and your shoes were red with Plainfield clay. Isn't that reason enough?'

'Quite,' I replied. 'But how in the name of conscience do you remember me?'

'Why, I *saw* you,' returned Crewe. 'Everybody within a twelve-mile radius of New York has seen everybody else — or at least, ninety percent of all other citizens, at some time. Need I remind you that on August 12, 1910, you took a small party to a roof garden on Forty-Second Street? Or that, the previous February, you rendered first aid to a child who'd been knocked down by a street car on Sixth Avenue?'

Later in the day, discovering Mr. Crewe alone in the smoking room, I showed him the photograph of a young man in cowboy attire and asked him if he could give me his history. He took the photograph and studied it intently, then closed his eyes in mental concentration.

'I've only seen this young fellow twice,' he said. 'Seven years ago he strolled up

Broadway from the Battery in a suit of English clothes, carrying a Gladstone bag. Three years afterward, while visiting New York from out west, he was arrested at the corner of Twenty-Third Street and Fifth Avenue on a charge of intoxication.'

I leaped from my seat. 'For the love of heaven, explain your secret to me,' I exclaimed. 'You may be the man I'm most in need of.'

Crewe smiled in a self-depreciatory manner. 'It's very simple,' he explained. 'You're no doubt aware of the discovery of psychologists that every mental image remains permanently impressed upon the brain?'

'Yes.'

'Unfortunately, when the average man sees a thing, he straightway forgets it. Similarly with what he hears. When you and I hear a passing sound — the scrape of a wave against the ship, the fall of a twig in the park — the impression is so faint that it's lost at once and never recurs to us throughout life. But when I receive an image through the eyes, I never forget it. In my earlier days it caused me a great

3

deal of inconvenience. Now, having acquired a modest competence and retired from business, I derive considerable amusement from this power. I travel, I study, I try to turn my advantage to the good of humanity. Already I may say that I know practically every inhabitant of New York City by sight and can recall every occasion on which I have ever seen him. I could tell you strange stories in this regard. I know half of London and two-thirds of Paris. Not a day passes but I meet a dozen old acquaintances, all of whom are blandly unconscious of having ever encountered me before.'

'But why should you not assist me?' I exclaimed. 'You're just the man I need to help me in unraveling a painful mystery.'

'I shall be delighted to be of service to you,' said Crewe. 'Let's be perfectly frank — that's all I ask.'

'I'll be *entirely* frank,' I answered. 'I'm traveling to England to investigate an affair which threatens the life of a man whom I believe to be innocent. Here's the story. Upon a small estate in Surrey there lived two brothers, retired Anglo-Indian officials. Both were widowers. Sir George Bamwell, the eldest, a baronet, had a daughter. His brother, William Bamwell, to whom the baronetcy would in due course descend, had a son — a ne'er-do-well who, after a rather profligate career, went off to America, where he became successively a sheep-herder, prospector, and cowboy. The boy was cast off by his father, a martinet of the old English school, and it was understood that the bulk of his money would go to Selim, an Indian servant, whom William Bamwell had brought home with him, and who'd served the brothers faithfully for twenty years.'

'The boy, I take it, is the original of the photograph you showed me,' said Crewe.

'Yes, and your statements in regard to him were perfectly correct. He did land in New York seven years ago, and he was arrested on a charge of intoxication at a subsequent date. Last year Claude Bamwell, the son, returned home unexpectedly. He'd tired of his roving life. He asked his father to give him another chance to redeem himself and to let him remain with him. The cousin, Lydia, the daughter of Sir George Bamwell, who had conceived a romantic attachment for her graceless relative, was instrumental in effecting a reconciliation between the father and son. Claude was given his chance and seemed to make good use of his opportunity. Within six months, father and son were on friendly terms. William Bamwell, who was perhaps seventy years of age, had a passion for amateur photography. Claude humored his father and never tired of helping him in his hobby. Father and son began to appreciate each other better than they'd ever done before.

'This increasing intimacy was not looked upon favorably by Selim, the Hindu servant, especially since William Bamwell contemplated altering his will in favor of his son, Claude, and greatly reducing the legacy which Selim had come to look upon as his own reversionary right. However, Selim was inscrutable and kept his own counsel.

'The Bamwell brothers were very set in their ways. One of the characteristics common to both of them was their fondness for a certain East Indian cigar that came from Borneo. These they imported direct from the manufacturer. Claude, however, discovered a similar brand on sale in London, and gave a box to his father for a Christmas present — at Selim's suggestion, as he declares. In fact, according to Claude, Selim discovered the existence of this brand and induced him to purchase the box. Selim, however, denies that he'd ever heard of these cigars and ascribes the entire scheme of purchasing and presenting them to Claude.

'Now we come to the crux of the situation. Three months ago Sir George Bamwell was discovered dead in the library early one morning. He'd been sitting up alone the night before, and had taken one of his brother's cigars — the first of the box. He was found dead, the half-smoked cigar upon the table before him. A post-mortem investigation disclosed the presence in the body of a minute portion of a powerful poison allied to prussic acid. The cigar was analyzed, but nothing was found wrong with it. In spite of a rigorous cross-examination of all persons concerned, no motive or clue could be discovered. Sir George was buried in the family vault, and William Bamwell became Sir William.

'Not three weeks afterward, the tragedy repeated itself. Sir William Bamwell was found dead in precisely the same manner. Again the presence of the prussic acid variant was disclosed at the post-mortem; again the cigar was analyzed and found to be entirely harmless. Yet Sir William, like his brother, had undoubtedly died after smoking half of the Borneo cigar.

'But in this case several new facts were brought out at the inquest. In the first place, Claude had been with his father until a few moments before his death. The two men had been smoking together. Sir William was a very rapid smoker; Claude preferred cigarettes and barely burned away an inch of his cigars, which he smoked merely to humor his father. Again, it was proved that Claude had recently purchased prussic acid at a drug show in the village. When interrogated, he acknowledged this fact, but asserted that his father used this deadly compound for intensifying the images upon negatives that had been underexposed. It's perfectly true that a certain compound of prussic acid is used for this purpose, and Sir William had always compounded his own photographic chemicals.

'To cut the story short, Claude — or Sir Claude, as I must now call him — was arrested on a charge of murder and is now awaiting trial at the assizes.'

'And the motive?' Crewe queried.

'Fear that his father, who was becoming a little senile, and was largely under the influence of Selim, would again disinherit him.'

'But did Claude know the contents of the will?'

'No. It had actually been changed in the son's favor, but so far as is known Sir William had kept his own counsel.'

'Then that works either way,' said Crewe. 'Selim might have committed the murder, fearing the will would be changed in the son's favor, and not knowing that this had actually been done. And that very open purchase of prussic acid is not compatible with guilt. And the cigars — how do they come into the story? You say that analysis showed them to be harmless?'

'Entirely so; and to my mind, whoever was the murderer, it wasn't Claude. But the young man had a bad name, and Selim appears to have made certain statements which greatly increased the feeling against him. However, all that is now *sub judice*.

'It was the cousin, Lydia, who at the instigation of Claude telegraphed to me to gather all material I could tending to show that the young man's life in America hadn't been so bad as is currently rumored in England, and to hurry across the water with this material to aid the defense. I may say that Claude Bamwell has never been convicted of a felony, and only once of a misdemeanor. I'm the attorney who defended him on the charge of intoxication.'

In this manner Crewe and I came to be associated in this first of our many enterprises.

I passed many an anxious moment until the boat docked at Tilbury. But all my speculations and impressions were killed abruptly when, at the moment of docking, a messenger rushed up and thrust a telegram into my hands. I tore it open and read:

'Claude Bamwell found guilty willful murder Godalming assizes. Judge refused postponement till your arrival, on ground your evidence not material. Come to Fairview instantly.'

Crewe shook his head dolefully when I showed him this missive. Although he wouldn't say so, I could see that he had scant hope in our ability to save Claude Bamwell's life. We took the train to Fenchurch Street and, half an hour later, were speeding southward in the Godalming local. At four that afternoon we arrived at Fairview, a small and unpretentious place, but in good taste and a typical English gentleman's country seat.

We found Mr. Clayton in charge. Lydia, the cousin, was prostrated and under medical care. Hardly had we taken our seats for a conference, however, than she appeared dramatically before us, arrayed in black, her hair disheveled, her eyes tear-stained.

'You must save Claude, Mr. Langton,'

she pleaded. 'Indeed, he never killed his father. Tell me that you haven't come all the way across the ocean fruitlessly.'

Slight as my hope was, I could not wholly cast it out. 'I'll do my best,' I said. 'I understand an appeal is to be taken to the court of criminal appeal. I can testify that the stories as to Claude's wild life in America are fabrications. I'll save him if he can be saved.'

Mr. Clayton took Lydia by the arm and led her to the door. 'We will spare no effort,' he said.

She seemed to collapse. Mr. Clayton led her to her room, while we waited in painful doubt. I saw Crewe cast his eye upon a photograph that stood upon the mantel. 'That's Selim, the Indian servant,' I explained to him. 'I had a duplicate copy of it, but unfortunately left it at home in the hurry of packing. Pleasant-looking fellow, isn't he?'

Crewe made no answer. His eyes were closed; he seemed to be calling up some memory. At this juncture Mr. Clayton returned and seated himself.

'Now, gentlemen,' he said briskly — I

had already introduced Mr. Crewe to him as my confidential assistant — 'I must confess that matters look very bleak indeed. In our English courts a conviction for murder is practically never reversed, and justice moves with appalling swiftness. Let me say, however, that I'm assured a hideous wrong has been done, and that the real criminal is the Indian. But for his perjured evidence, a very different verdict would have been returned.

'What most impressed the jury was the fact that a prussic acid compound was found in the bodies of both Sir George and Sir William, while it was proved that Claude had bought prussic acid at the village drug store. Then there was the motive — fear that the will would be revoked. But what clinched the jurors in their decision was Selim's evidence that Claude had approached him with the project of destroying his father and sharing the money that might be left, irrespective of the will. Selim had been a faithful servant for many years; Claude was reputed to have been a man of vilest character in America. The judge, who is old and testy, refused to wait until you could put in evidence in rebuttal of this, on the ground that it was immaterial in law. Perhaps it was — but in fact it undoubtedly decided the jury's verdict.'

'And where's Selim?' I asked.

'Living at the village hotel,' said Mr. Clayton. 'Living there brazenly. Says he'll remain on the spot until his dear master has been avenged, and is the object of universal solicitude, as Sir Claude is of execration.'

'And now,' I said, 'what part did the cigars play in this mystery?'

'None whatever,' answered Mr. Clayton.

'Have you the rest of the box?'

'No,' Mr. Clayton answered. 'Oddly enough, it can't be found. It disappeared on the day of the murder, together with the bulk of the prussic acid supposed to have been purchased, and with a few other little articles having relation to the crime. But none of these is material. The prosecuting attorney suggested that Claude had hidden these in an effort to destroy all evidence of his crime.'

'Can we see this Selim?' asked Peter Crewe.

'Well,' said Mr. Langton, 'if you think

it'll do any good, we can undoubtedly find him at the village hotel.'

At Crewe's urging we started out for the village. It was a small country town of one main street, flanked by little laborers' cottages, with here and there a tradesman's residence of more imposing type. At the inn we learned that Selim was out walking.

'What time does the next train come in from Godalming?' Crewe asked.

'At seven minutes past five,' the landlord answered.

'And departs?'

'There's a twelve-past local running clear through to Charing Cross.'

'We have just time to catch the local,' said Crewe, looking at his watch. 'Mr. Clayton, we leave you here and shall see you tomorrow.' Then, disregarding the lawyer's look of surprise, he took me by the arm and, without further explanation, urged me to accompany him. I saw that something important must have transpired.

'This fellow Selim doesn't know you by sight?' he asked.

'No,' I said.

'Still, it would be as well not to let him

perceive two strangers when he arrives on the down-platform.'

'But where are we going?' I asked.

'Tilbury,' said Crewe shortly. 'There's no time to lose. With your permission, I'll defer explanations until later.'

We reached the station with three minutes to spare. As we panted up the inclined pathway toward the train, Crewe pulled me aside into the shadows of a cluster of box cars. An instant later I saw Selim pass stealthily by in the direction of the village. He had evidently arrived on the down train.

Still amazed, I entered the up train and, as soon as we were settled in our compartment, Crewe turned to me. 'I think, Mr. Langton,' he said, 'that we shall find that box of cigars in that rag and bone shop along the waterfront of Tilbury. Doubtless you remember it.'

'But — ' I began.

'Did you not see this Selim entering it this morning as we came to anchorage?' Crewe asked.

'I remember an Asiatic with a parcel entering some shop.'

16

'You couldn't distinguish the face? It was rather faint. Nevertheless, that man was the original of the photograph upon the mantel at Fairview, and the parcel was a box of cigars wrapped in a dirty cloth. Selim must have learned of our coming and determined to remove all evidence from the scene of the crime. Not daring to burn or bury the cigars, he resolved to go to London secretly and dispose of the box to some one of his compatriots who frequent the Wapping and Tilbury purlieus. By great good fortune his visit synchronized with our arrival.'

At Crewe's suggestion we purchased cloth caps and threw away our felt hats; we turned up the collars of our coats and made ourselves appear as much as possible in our role of ship's officers ashore. Finding the junk shop was easy. As Crewe had surmised, it was kept by an East Indian, a swarthy, ill-favored fellow who eyed us with no very great appreciation.

'Mate,' said Crewe, 'we want some smokes to take aboard with us in the morning.'

Without a word the East Indian produced a handful of vile-looking cheroots.

Crewe tossed them roughly aside.

'What d'ye take me for?' he said somewhat thickly, as though slightly under the influence of liquor. 'Gimme a box. Got any split boxes?'

Leaning over the counter, I saw a small package wrapped up in a dirty cloth, which disclosed the end of a cigar box. 'Gimme *those*,' I said, pointing.

The East Indian looked at me furtively. He took up the box, unwrapped the cloth — and suddenly darted through the back door of his shop. Instantly Crewe leaped upon him.

'*Hold him!*' he cried to me, as the Indian twisted himself adroitly out of Crewe's grasp. I saw his hand go down to his side and, with an unfortunate blow, knocked my colleague sprawling. His head came in contact with the edge of the door and the fall stunned him. The box fell from his clasp. Picking it up hastily, I saw upon the cover the word 'Borneo.'

'*Come on!*' cried Crewe, and holding the box under my coat, I darted after him down the alley. We reached the main road panting, and finding that we were not pursued, set off at a rapid pace toward the station. On the way we recovered our hats, which we had thrown behind some boarding.

★   ★   ★

It was five o'clock on the following morning when we reached Fairview, after many hours of waiting at junctions for trains which either didn't run, or did so with exasperating unpunctuality. We went straight to the house and called Mr. Clayton out of bed. Crewe held up the cigars.

'Now, Mr. Clayton, we must act quickly,' he said, 'or you'll find that the quarry has flown. Can you bring Selim to the house as soon as possible?'

'I'll do so at once,' said Mr. Clayton, much mystified.

'If he refuses to come — ' I said.

'He won't refuse. I can procure a warrant from Mr. Tighe, our nearest magistrate. But may I ask — '

'I would rather say nothing,' Crewe answered. 'It's a desperate hope, and yet it seems built upon something of a foundation. At any rate, it won't do any harm. May I be allowed the setting of the little drama?'

'By all means,' Mr. Clayton answered.

He set off as soon as he had snatched a hasty breakfast of bread and milk, and after two hours of waiting, Crewe and I saw him reappear with Selim. The servant came in blandly; he was as suave in his demeanor as he had been pictured, though I thought I could discern an uneasy glance in his eye.

'Sit down, Mr. Selim,' said Mr. Clayton. 'These gentlemen are friends of Claude Bamwell and wish to interrogate you.'

'I shall be delighted to do everything in my power to assist them,' said the Indian, seating himself easily at the table. 'If only I could believe that the unhappy young man was not guilty of my dear master's death — '

'Do you *smoke*, Mr. Selim?' asked Crewe abruptly.

The Indian started violently; then, recovering his composure, replied: 'I am not much of a smoker, sir.'

'But you *have* smoked? Will you oblige me by smoking a cigar with me?' And he produced the box of Borneos.

I never saw such a change come over a human countenance as came over the Indian's. For a moment he gasped like a fish out of water. Before he could regain his self-possession, Crewe had placed before him a sheet of paper and a pencil. Upon the paper was written: 'I swear that I and I alone am responsible for the death of my master, Sir George Bamwell.'

'As an alternative to smoking, perhaps you'll sign this,' said Crewe. 'You may do both,' he added.

The Indian collapsed into his chair with a ghastly smile. 'No, I will smoke,' he said, pushing the paper away.

Crewe calmly lit a cigar, and then applied a match to the Indian's. And there they sat, smoking in perfect silence, while we others gathered around in strained expectancy.

'Come, throw away your cigar, Selim, and sign that paper,' said Crewe after a pause. The Indian's cigar now had an inch of ash on it; Crewe's was hardly rimmed.

Suddenly, as if inspired by some invincible determination, the Indian began smoking furiously. The smoke came from his mouth in puffs. His cigar was half-consumed. The silence deepened. Some dreadful tragedy seemed to depend upon the issue of that smoking match.

'Selim,' said Crewe, laying down his cigar, 'sign that paper.' And he removed the cigar from the Indian's mouth.

I saw the Indian shoot out a trembling claw. He grasped the pencil and wrote his name almost illegibly beneath the paper. Then he glanced into our faces with a pitiful smile. 'It is finished,' he said, and picked up the cigar again.

Crewe leaped toward him and tried to wrest the cigar from his mouth. But the Indian, with a grip of steel, held Crewe's wrists, all the while drawing in and puffing out the smoke in thick clouds. The ash was lengthening. Still none of us stirred. We were fascinated into inertia by this strange drama.

All at once the end came. I saw an

ashen pallor overspread Selim's swarthy face. He choked; he beat the air with his hands; then, without a sound, he toppled over to the ground. Mr. Clayton raised him quickly, but one look into Selim's face was sufficient to tell us all that life was ended.

'You see, gentlemen,' said Crewe, 'as I suspected, those cigars were highly charged with a volatile poison, a variant of prussic acid. Selim had given the box to Claude to present to his father; or, rather, had cunningly contrived that Claude should purchase the box at the store in Tilbury, where he'd it placed on sale. The reason why no poison was found in the cigar butts was that it had already been drawn out of the cigars into the lungs of the victims.

'You know that as one smokes a cigar toward the butt, the stump constantly becomes warmer and damper, the fluids being driven back by the flame. There was no danger in the cigars until they were half-smoked down, as the poison didn't vaporize. After they were half-smoked, however, the acid became sufficiently heated to pass into vapor, which was inhaled into the smoker's lungs and caused immediate death. It was a diabolical trick, and could only have originated in the cunning mind of an East Indian, a race notorious for its vendettas and vengeances.'

'And if you hadn't so opportunely seen Selim entering the shop at Tilbury?' I suggested. 'The coincidence was almost an impossible one, according to the laws of chance — and yet it saved an innocent life.'

'There are no laws of chance,' Crewe answered. 'Believe me, Langton, somewhere or other lies the clue to every crime, if only one has sense to discern it.'

2

The Robbery at the Tower

After the adventure of the Box of Borneos, which I've already described, and which Peter Crewe was enabled to solve by his peculiar optical powers, we struck up a warm friendship. It was arranged that we should work together in the future for the solution of any similar difficulties which might come to me in the course of my professional career. We had arranged to catch the next steamship for America, but on the day before she sailed, there occurred in London a robbery of such a mysterious character that neither of us could resist the temptation to remain and lend our aid to the discovery of the criminal.

Everybody remembers how the famous Gwyn jewels were stolen from the Tower of London. These emeralds, which had a historic rather than any especial intrinsic value, had been presented by Charles II to his famous favorite. They were preserved in a small chamber in the Tower, where were stored miscellaneous treasures of secondary importance not usually placed on public exhibition. They were kept in an isolated building, a round turret which ran straight up to a height of seventy feet, and was absolutely inaccessible from the outside, the brick walls affording not the slightest foothold. In fact there was no direct access to this tower at all, since it connected with the main building by a series of passageways, intricate, and entirely unapproachable except from the central building 200 yards away, which was guarded by a file of soldiers. This turret had a small barrel window overlooking the road, 60 feet up. It was too high for any thief to throw up a grappling hook; in short nothing but a fireman's ladder could have gained access to it from the outside.

Yet in spite of this, the window *was* entered from the outside, a bar was removed from the mortar setting, and the thief gained entrance, obtained possession of the emeralds, and calmly descended unobserved. The robbery wasn't discovered until the following day, by which time the perpetrator of the crime had got safely away.

The daring nature of the crime excited all London. It was certain that no ladder had been used to gain admittance. While the tower was unguarded, persons were continually passing and repassing in the road beneath, and any such device would have been speedily detected, the more so inasmuch as any ladder placed against the wall would have been set at such an angle that it would have blocked the sidewalk underneath.

On the third day after the robbery, the emeralds were discovered in the pawn shop of a notorious fence in Whitechapel region. They'd been left there by an Italian, the man confessed when threatened with prosecution. Neighbors of the pawnbroker confirmed his statement. An itinerant organ-grinder, accompanied by a monkey, had been seen to enter the pawn shop on the day after the robbery. His monkey seemed to be sick, one neighbor added. It was wrapped in blankets and lay listlessly on the top of the organ. It was an extremely large animal, and those who saw it had received the impression that it was a chimpanzee, though nothing of it could be seen, since it was swathed from head to foot.

Other witnesses confirmed this statement. It was, furthermore, known that an Italian organ-grinder had been seen in the vicinity of the Tower for several days before the robbery. Although he'd chosen the worst place for the plying of his trade, and had taken in practically nothing, he'd cheerfully ground out his tunes day after day at the base of the turret. His monkey, however, lay on the top of the organ, just as the other witnesses had described, and never stirred a muscle. Some children who had tried to pet it were angrily shooed away by the organ-grinder, who asserted that the animal was sick.

That was all that could be learned. All the itinerant organ-grinders in London were promptly investigated by the police, but no man with such an animal was found. Although the jewels had been recovered, fear of other daring robberies of a similar kind impelled the authorities to prosecute their search in the most vigorous manner.

'The first thing to do,' said Crewe to me when we'd agreed to do our best to unravel the mystery, 'is to look at the turret.'

We went thither accordingly and found a curious crowd standing in a solid phalanx at the base of the tower, gazing up at the brick walls, while a couple of policemen stolidly moved them on whenever their numbers became too great for street traffic to pass. It seemed impossible that anyone could have scaled those walls without a ladder.

'Do you suppose the man sent his monkey up?' I hazarded.

Crewe smiled and shook his head. 'A monkey might possibly be able to find a foothold in the bricks,' he said. 'But how could it have sawn out the iron bar? Apart from this, no monkey could be trained to bring down any article its trainer wished for. No, Langton, ingenious as your theory is, we must dismiss it from the realms of possibility.'

The sun was shining — a rare thing in London — and Crewe, having carefully inspected the base of the walls, now fell back to some distance and proceeded to take them in as a whole. He fixed both eyes unwinkingly upon the tower, so that every detail should impress itself upon either retina.

'And now,' said Crewe, 'we'll take our photograph from the other side.' And we moved round, and once again he focused his eyes upon the brickwork.

'That's all,' he said as the sun went behind a cloud. 'I think the discovery won't prove to be as difficult as it appears.'

'Hindeed!' said one of the policemen on duty, who overheard this remark. 'May I ask, sir, if you can furnish any clue?'

'Tell the governor of the tower,' said Crewe, smiling, 'that the robbery wasn't committed by an Italian at all, but by a South American, whom you people would doubtless confuse with Italians.'

'A South American!' repeated the other policeman stolidly. 'And doubtless, sir, his monkey was also a South American,' he continued with clumsy sarcasm.

'You're quite right,' said Crewe calmly. 'His monkey wasn't a monkey, but it certainly was a South American.'

'And you get all this from hinspecting the brick walls, sir?' the policeman asked.

'Every bit,' said Crewe.

'You don't 'appen to know more about this affair than you've told us, sir?' said the policeman.

I pulled Crewe away. 'If you awaken suspicion in the minds of the addle-pates, you'll find yourself arrested on suspicion,' I whispered.

We moved off, the policeman following us with suspicious glances. It was not until we were upon the outskirts of the crowd that I breathed freely. 'Crewe,' I said, 'it won't do to prod the British policeman. Now tell me, were you serious in what you said about the South American and his monkey?'

'I was never more serious,' Crewe answered. 'But I said that it wasn't a monkey. Tell me, Langton, what you saw on the tower.'

'I saw a series of well-fitted bricks,' I

answered, 'offering a good foothold for a fly and possibly for a small monkey, but certainly not for a man.'

'But what did you see on the bricks in the shape of markings?'

'A few mosses, which some scientist might label and classify.'

'*Tush!*' said Crewe petulantly. '*This* is what *I* saw.' He stopped, produced a pencil and a piece of paper from his pocket, and began to trace a series of three-pointed marks like hen's tracks. 'There was a well-ordered series of these,' he said, 'commencing upon the nineteenth layer of bricks from the bottom, and thence running, with a slightly oblique movement, clear up to the window.' He closed his eyes. 'I'm looking at them now,' he continued. 'At intervals corresponding roughly to every four of these tracks, there are slight but well-defined depressions in the surface having the rough outline of a shoe. Fragments of brick have crumbled here and there under the pressure of hobnails. In other words, Langton, our South American friend *did* ascend that turret, walking up its surface as a fly might walk. What's the inference?'

'That he threw a rope up over the bars and climbed, pulling himself up hand over hand. Therefore he's a sailor,' I said with a sudden light.

Crewe looked at me in great amusement. 'My dear Sherlock Holmes, you're quite wrong,' he answered. 'Ingenious, but speculative. We're dealing in exactitudes, and there's no possible evidence to show that the man threw up a rope or is a sailor.'

At the juncture a newsboy came past yelling a special edition of an evening newspaper. 'Murder at Notting Hill! Murder at Notting Hill! Full description of scenes of horror,' the vendor called. Crewe stopped to purchase a copy, unfolded the damp sheet, and read from under a staring headline.

'A dastardly murder was committed in the early hours of this morning at Notting Hill. The residence of Mr. Walter Deans, a retired tradesman, was entered, and valuables to the amount of more than a thousand pounds were taken, and the owner was shot down while endeavoring, as is supposed, to defend his home. The body of Mr. Deans was discovered by his servants about eleven o'clock lying across the fireplace in his bedroom, which was in confusion, as though it had been minutely ransacked. No clue has yet been discovered as to the identity of the murderer, although a foreign-looking man had been observed lurking in the vicinity recently. Mr. Deans' house stands alone in extensive grounds; it is a perfectly plain brick structure, and the robber appears to have entered through the window of the third story, on which is Mr. Deans' bedroom, though how he contrived to effect an entrance without foothold remains for the present a mystery.

'I suspected as much,' said Crewe. 'The fellow is so emboldened by the success of his first attempt that unless he's caught, a series of crimes will follow. We must get him this afternoon.'

'You think it was the same man?'

'Undoubtedly,' said Crewe. 'But to make sure, let's take the train for Notting Hill immediately.'

We arrived there an hour and a half

later. The grounds were packed with an immense throng, whom the police were ineffectually endeavoring to disperse. Crewe stopped and focused his eyes upon the building.

'What's your business 'ere?' demanded a policeman roughly. 'Move on there!'

Crewe turned abruptly and left the grounds. 'The same tracks,' he muttered. 'Now, Langton, we must catch this fellow tonight.'

'Will you not tell me the significance of the markings?' I asked.

'Not now, Langton. I want to bend every effort to apprehending the murderer. Luckily it won't be difficult. Since the police imagine him to be an Italian, he won't have any incentive to disguise his true nationality. You know the Spanish quarter?'

'Bloomsbury,' I said.

'We shall find him there. These people would rather die than live outside their own neighborhoods. Watch for a man with a sack.'

'A *sack*?' I queried.

'Yes,' said Crewe impatiently. 'He

wouldn't dare to maintain the organ-grinder fiction; nor will he venture to leave the creature in his room. We must search the streets until we find him.'

At Tottenham Court Road we took an omnibus and, seated upon the roof, observed the streets below. Nothing escaped Crewe's observant eyes. When we had passed through the Bloomsbury district, we descended. Crewe hailed a hansom, and for an hour or more we drove slowly up and down the squalid thoroughfares, Crewe's eyes registering every human being among the mass of pedestrians. Suddenly he signaled to the driver and leaped out.

'Follow that man!' he exclaimed.

In front of us, some two hundred yards' distance, a swarthy fellow of Spanish or Italian origin was strolling leisurely through the streets. He was attired in the corduroys and overalls of a working man and had a small sack slung over one shoulder.

'We mustn't let him escape,' Crewe muttered. It was growing dark, and we hastened our footsteps until we were almost abreast of him. Then we followed him, now on this side of the road, now upon that, while he pursued his course through Bloomsbury, into Seven Dials, thence through Covent Garden and along the waste of half-erected buildings on Kingsway, the county council thoroughfare. At a signal from Crewe we fell back a little.

'How do you know he's the man?' I questioned hurriedly.

'He bears the mark of the beast,' Crewe returned.

'The beast?'

'Look at his collar.'

I crept up more closely and suddenly perceived, upon the cheap celluloid collar that the man wore, the identical hen-track — three finger marks, clearly outlined — that Crewe had drawn upon the paper. A sudden sense of horror almost overcame me. I fell back again and waited for Crewe to join me. 'What are you going to do?' I whispered.

'Seize him — at an opportune moment.'

It was night now, and the thoroughfare, which was not yet installed with street lamps, was so dark that we could discern our man only as a shadow moving among shadows. He stopped before the flank of a new building from little cells in whose walls lights gleamed fitfully. I knew it to be one of the county council structures for the housing of poor persons, but could not imagine for what purpose the robber intended breaking in.

He hesitated a moment, then moved round toward the end of the block. And suddenly I was enlightened. As though emerging out of squalor into fairyland, I saw before me the splendid new Wemyss Hotel, fronting upon the Strand. Now the robber's purpose was made clear. If he could ascend that blank wall of the lodging house for fifty feet and more — if, like a fly, he could climb that apparently impassable structure — he could gain the unlit back court of the hotel and have each tier of rooms at his mercy, while their occupants were dining or enjoying themselves at some place of entertainment. It was a daring conception, for the enclosed courtyard, dominated by a bare brick wall, was wholly unguarded, being deemed un-enterable.

As we crouched in the shadows we saw the robber glance swiftly round. The thoroughfare was apparently deserted; nobody was likely to pass through on any honest purpose. Stealthily he opened the sack, plunged in his arm, and drew out some furry creature of large size — a monkey, and yet *not* a monkey, for instead of chattering and leaping this thing lay apparently lifeless in his arms. The man deposited it carefully in a recess between two angles of the building and then began pulling out of the bag what seemed like an unending cord.

'By God, I was right!' I heard Crewe mutter. I was trembling with excitement; yet for the life of me I could not see what the man intended to do.

Presently he appeared to come to the end of the cord. He pulled off his coat and waistcoat and made it fast around his waist. Then, picking up the creature in his arms, he placed it against the side of the building.

To my astonishment the thing began to move. The strange black creature climbed higher and higher against the blank wall of the lodging house. Higher and higher yet it went, apparently walking upon the perpendicular slope, until the topmost window was attained. Then I saw the burglar jerk the rope. The animal disappeared. A moment afterward he was hauling himself up the wall, hand over hand, with perfect ease and apparently perfect security.

Crewe crept forward and drew a revolver from his pocket. '*Halt!*' he said quietly to the man in the air. 'Halt, or I fire. Come down!'

I saw a struggle upon the perpendicular wall. The clinging man grasped at the rope, missed it, seemed to lose his foothold, and suddenly fell some twenty feet in the air. The loose rope tightened with an awful shock; the body quivered an instant, and then began to swing like a pendulum from side to side along the flank of the building. At every turn the rope rose higher around him. It was slipping upward from his waist, where he had fastened it, toward his throat, one arm having slipped through the noose in the struggle. At every turn the body assumed an attitude more and more perpendicular.

Finally, with a sudden shock, the noose slipped round the neck and the corpse swung evenly at the rope's end, the vibrations gradually lessening until the body hung limp and loose and lifeless, its one free arm dangling, the other pinned by the rope to the neck, the forearm waving weakly around the head. Nothing that we could have done could have saved him. Twenty feet at least above our heads that dreadful drama was enacted in the air.

'He has but anticipated his fate,' said Crewe. 'Poor devil! His ingenuity undid him. Let's go, Langton; there is no purpose to be served by our remaining here.'

On the following morning all London was agape over the latest mystery. A policeman, according to the account, had found the body of a man suspended from an upper window of a tenement house by a rope of prodigious length. He had cut him down, but the suicide had evidently been dead for several hours. The rope was ingeniously knotted around the window bars; yet it had not been fastened from within, the window bolted and the room having been unoccupied for more than a week previously.

Another item in the same newspaper passed without notice; yet the two were indissolubly connected.

'Early this morning,' it ran, 'while going to work, John Jarvis, a plumber, noticed a strange beast in the Strand. It was suspended from a window sill, and at first seemed to be dead, but was subsequently found to be sleeping. The beast was noosed and taken to the police station, where it was discovered, after some investigation, to be a harmless sloth of the armadillo type. Its final destination will probably be the Zoological Gardens.'

Crewe looked up at me. 'The greatest mystery,' he said, 'is how the creature contrived to knot the rope round the window bars so that it held up the body of the burglar after it had departed upon its nocturnal prowlings in search of food.'

'Crewe,' I said, 'you haven't explained *anything* of the mystery to me as yet. I don't know how the burglar entered the tower, *nor* how you knew him to be a South American, *nor* the meaning of the hen-tracks.'

Crewe started. 'My dear Langton, forgive me,' he pleaded. 'I'll do so at once. Do you know anything about the habits of the sloth?'

'I'd never heard of such an animal before today,' I answered.

'Just so,' Crewe answered, smiling. 'Now if you, an educated American, know nothing of this animal, it's safe to say that nobody else does, except, here and there, some naturalist. Isn't it reasonable, therefore, to assume that the man who owned it was intimately acquainted with it — in other words that he was a denizen of South America, the continent in which the sloth has its habitat? And if that deduction weren't logical enough, we have the testimony of the pawnbroker and his neighbors to the effect that the man was an Italian — the generic term in England for all southerners of swarthy complexion.'

'Yes,' I said, 'granted the sloth, I will

admit that its owner was probably a South American. But what gave you the idea of its being a sloth, and how does it come into the story?'

'Why,' said Crewe, 'I saw its marks upon the brickwork of the tower, and also at Notting Hill. The sloth has only three toes, and its marks are as much like hen-tracks as anything in the world. You've undoubtedly seen a sloth's feet at the Zoological Gardens when you were a boy.'

'Undoubtedly; but they entirely escaped my recollection.'

'That's the difference between us,' said Crewe, smiling. 'But, to continue, the sloth has acquired the remarkable habit of hanging by its toes from the branches of trees. With its head down, its heavy body suspended by its slender paws, it sleeps happily all through the day, awakening only at night, when it pursues its insect prey. When suspended in this manner, *nothing* can dislodge it; in fact, the sloth seems able to defy the laws of gravity. A weight of a ton, affixed to its body, wouldn't pull it downward or disturb it in its ecstatic slumbers. On the other hand, by unclasping the paws and pulling upward, the sloth can be easily and harmlessly removed from its resting place.

'And so our organ-grinder had a sloth in place of a monkey. The plan of displaying it in the streets openly, under the guise of a sick monkey, was a brilliant conception, and shows us that our criminal was a man of a high degree of mentality.

'The rest of the picture, Langton, you can fill in for yourself. Having discovered the most convenient hour for his enterprise, the burglar attaches a long rope around the creature, coiling the other end around his body, and places it upon the wall. Our sloth, feeling the smooth surface beneath him, and being unable to sleep perpendicularly, conceives the idea that he's upon the stem of a peculiarly high and smooth palm tree, at whose summit he may hope to find a comfortable branch from which it is his delight to feed. He ascends as long as the rope holds out. When he reaches the level of the window, his master maneuvers him against the bars, feeling which, and imagining them to be branches, the sloth promptly fastens himself by the feet, lets his head fall, and passes into a delicious slumber.

'We now have our sloth firmly affixed to the bars. No weight pulling from below can dislodge him. In other words, the burglar has anchored his rope outside the window of the room to which he desires to gain admittance. Now, aided by darkness of one of these perpetual London fogs, he ascends the rope, bracing himself against the brick walls, reaches his destination, effects his haul, and then descends in the same way, afterward pulling down the animal, probably through some slip-knot arrangement. It was a most ingenious contrivance, Langton, and if our robber had not wrongly adjusted his rope, so that it slipped round his throat and strangled him, he might have scrambled up out of reach and managed to elude us.'

3

The Tell-Tale Glove

The arrival in New York of Sir Moresby Blount was widely chronicled in the newspapers. Sir Moresby was a self-made Englishman who, starting in life in the humble capacity of an itinerant vegetable vendor, had become first a merchant prince, then a company promoter, and finally a millionaire, having a mansion in Park Lane and interests in a dozen ventures all over the globe. Thousands of poor investors blessed him when his companies declared their annual dividends of twelve and fifteen percent. In his coronation year the late king had knighted him. And now, immensely prosperous, pompous and self-sufficient, Sir Moresby had come to America 'to hinterest meself in the development of your magnificent but unprogressive west,' as he phrased it to the reporters who met him when the ship docked in New York harbor.

Mining ventures were the cause of Sir Moresby's visit to America. He proposed to develop 'all the mineral resources of Harizona, including bismuth, copper, and hantimony.' If Sir Moresby's aitches were a trifle superfluous, his pocketbook was evidently in the right place. He was condescendingly affable to his visitors, and, after registering at the New Hague Hotel, announced his intention of 'doing' the town alone, in order to rediscover America.

His little rat-like English secretary, who had accompanied him, afterward conducted the reporters to the magnificent offices in a Fifth Avenue building, which had just been opened to accommodate the American branch of Sir Moresby's business, and where two dozen recently employed clerks were busily opening letters and filing applications for shares along the sides of the new mahogany table.

It was with astonishment, therefore, that on opening my morning paper on the day after the millionaire's arrival, I saw in great black headlines the announcement of his death. He had gone out alone to 'rediscover America' on the preceding evening, and when he did not return shortly before midnight, his secretary became alarmed and telephoned the police. Within two hours his body was brought into the morgue, dripping wet from the cold waters of the East River. The skull was fractured and the face beaten almost out of all recognition; but the clothes identified the man beyond all doubt. Sir Moresby had evidently been struck down from behind while prowling in the unsavory purlieus of the East Side, robbed of money, watch and chain and jewelry, and flung into the stream, which washed him ashore opportunely in the vicinity of the police patrol station.

Hardly had I laid down the paper when there came a ring at my telephone. I took the receiver off the hook and heard the agitated voice of the general manager of the Salamander Life Insurance Company, for which I acted as lawyer.

'Langton,' he called, 'have you seen the account of the murder of Sir Moresby Blount?'

'Yes,' I called back. 'What of it?'

'*What of it?* My God, Langton, he insured last month with our English branch for *two hundred and fifty thousand dollars*!'

Ten minutes later the manager was in my office, urging me to look into the matter. There might be some mistake, he said. It might be suicide, in which case the policy would be invalidated. There might be some flaw in the policy, or the premiums might have lapsed. They had cabled to their English branch; meanwhile would I proceed to the New Hague Hotel and see the dead man's secretary?

I summoned Peter Crewe over the telephone. If there were any mystery, Crewe could clear it up. With his wonderful optical powers — which had already helped me in solving many a mystery I can never possibly recount — I knew that I could have chosen no better confidant.

I met him by appointment at the door of his hotel. Crewe, however, was not disposed to see any prospect of helping the company. 'It looks like a clear case of murder, Langton,' he said, 'and between you and me, I don't want to help them evade their responsibilities.'

'But you'll come with me?' I urged.

'Gladly,' said Crewe. 'And if there's any legitimate way in which I can serve your interests, you may count on me.'

At the entrance to the New Hague Hotel we ran into the little secretary, Randall, whom I recognized from his photograph, which had been published in the newspapers. I had expected that he would not be overzealous in assisting me, but to my surprise he placed himself at my service in the most cordial manner.

'I have to go back to the morgue,' he said, 'and you'd better come along with me. There is, I'm sorry to say, no doubt but that the body is that of Sir Moresby. Even if I couldn't swear to the features — which I am prepared to — the clothes would prove the identity beyond all possibility of doubt.'

It was no pleasant sight to see the millionaire, lately so self-sufficient, now compressed into that 'narrow measure of a man.' Crewe, standing beside me, looked hard upon the battered features. Then, reverently, but with a certain incongruity of action which surprised me even at the time, he took one of the dead man's hands in his, turned it palm upward, and passed his own hands lightly and caressingly across it.

'You're satisfied as to the identity, Mr. Langton?' asked Randall, the secretary.

'I see no reason to doubt it,' I answered. 'I can assure you that the Salamander Life Insurance Company isn't likely to withhold payment upon the ground that proof of death is missing. The evidence of identity appears conclusive, and after the compliance with a few formalities the money will be turned over to the executors. And now, if your lawyer is at hand, I should like to go through the form of inspecting the dead man's papers.'

'Of course, of course,' said Randall — a little nervously, I thought. 'We can do no more good here; let's return to the New Hague Hotel.'

My purpose was merely to discover whether the dead man had paid his premiums regularly; the remainder of his affairs did not concern me. I found the insurance papers in good order, and that the policy had been made out 'to estate.' Randall, as the executor, would therefore receive the $250,000.

'Did Sir Moresby have a photograph?' asked Crewe as we sat in the millionaire's rooms and looked through his belongings.

'He didn't bring any to this country,' said Randall. 'But, of course, there are the newspaper snapshots,' he added, 'if you want one.'

While we talked, I perceived that Crewe was wandering, a little restlessly, around the room. Once or twice he halted and seemed to be inspecting some of the personal belongings of Sir Moresby closely. Upon a small table lay an old pair of gloves of thin kid, and unlined. I was astonished to see Crewe slip one of these into his pocket while Randall's back was turned.

There seemed no more to be done. I went away and reported to the general manager of the Salamander that payment ought to be made, subject to the two weeks of delay that the policy provided for. There seemed to be no mystery in the case at all.

I was therefore considerably surprised when Crewe telephoned me that afternoon to come over at once, but first to telephone the Salamander people to postpone payment for a couple of weeks. As this was to be done in any event, I did not find it necessary to take up the subject with the general manager again, but went straight to Crewe's apartments, which were situated in a modest block upon Twenty-Second Street. I found him at the door, his hands dripping with purple dye.

'What on earth have you been doing?' I asked.

Then I perceived that a great bowl of the dye stood in the center of his table, in which floated Sir Moresby's glove, turned inside out and of an intense purple hue.

'Langton,' he said, 'we must have Randall watched ceaselessly until the moment of his departure for Arizona.'

'How do you know he's going to Arizona?' I asked.

'Because Sir Moresby can't go now,'

said Crewe; the jest appeared a little out of place to me. 'Can you have your company make out a check to him for the full amount and immediately telephone to the bank suspending payment?'

'It could be done,' I said. 'But unless there was an urgent reason for such a course of action, it would lead to most unpleasant complications.'

'Nevertheless, it's the only way,' said Crewe. 'Randall will loaf around New York until he gets the money. He won't disclose his hand until the ultimate moment. All our detective work must be done in the interval between the reception of the check and the presentation of it for payment. He won't wait a moment longer after the check has been received.'

'Do you mean to suggest that he murdered Sir Moresby for the insurance?' I queried.

'In a way — yes,' said Crewe. 'We must have detectives upon his trail every moment henceforward.'

'The police — '

'Emphatically *not*,' said Crewe. 'A private agency, which will not be tempted to play up the sensational possibilities and will know enough to keep their mouths shut. It's essential that Randall should suspect nothing. And I think that on the day of payment we'll be able to arrest the gang of conspirators.'

That was all I could get him to say. That same evening a couple of detectives were placed upon Randall's trail, with instructions to shadow him wherever he went. Meanwhile I arranged with the Salamander Company to pay the check upon the fourteenth day, and immediately suspend payment.

'He won't get in touch with his confederates until the check has actually been received,' said Crewe. 'Nevertheless, if there's anything to be learned, it'll be as well to have him shadowed.'

But as we expected, nothing came of the shadowing. Randall attended the funeral of the dead man on the third day afterward, attired in deepest black and wearing an air of intense dejection. He gave up his apartments at the New Hague Hotel and took cheaper lodging further uptown. Promptly every day at eleven he entered the gorgeous new suite of offices, where the clerks worked at the mahogany tables. The death of the millionaire had apparently not affected public confidence in the Arizona development scheme, for advertisements in heavy type continued to appear in the newspapers and subscriptions flowed in.

Upon the fourteenth day it was my duty to appear at the offices in person with the check for the insurance money, which I duly paid over to Randall. There was a furtive look in his eyes when he received it. Signing the receipt, he ushered me out of the place with affected bonhomie; then, turning as I waited for the elevator, I saw him catch his overcoat nervously from the hook on which it was hung, and I knew by some instinctive process of thought that it was his intention never again to enter the sumptuous offices. A sudden conviction came over me that the whole affair was a gigantic fraud; that the Salamander had been victimized by a set of unscrupulous swindlers who had not hesitated at murder to achieve their ends. Randall, the head and front of the conspiracy, was yet only a pliant tool in their hands.

By prearrangement, Crewe was to have been waiting for me at the foot of the elevator. It was a large building containing some dozen floors, all packed with offices; beneath, three telephone operators were busy at their boards, while a number of small telephone booths accommodated those who wished to communicate with other parts of the town.

In place of Crewe I found awaiting me an inspector of the telephone company, wearing the distinctive hat of his office. I gazed at him; something about his appearance seemed familiar. Suddenly I perceived that this *was* Crewe, but he had shaved off his mustache, and his whole facial appearance seemed to be changed. He saw my recognition of him and gave me the slightest look of warning.

Crewe advanced toward the telephone boards and planted himself between two of the operators. 'You have a call from 867 Sixth Avenue,' he said. This was Randall's office number.

'For 8214 Harlem,' one of the operators responded.

'Get me the street and number immediately,' said Crewe. 'Get into the booth,' he continued to me in a whisper.

I had hardly slipped into the booth nearest me before I saw Randall step out of the elevator and, after glancing secretively around in order to make sure that he was not followed, hurry out into the street.

'I'm trying to get Central, sir,' said the operator to Crewe.

'Hurry them up,' said Crewe.

A moment later Central responded. 'The number is 246 Wilcox Avenue,' said the operator.

Without a word Crewe hurried into the street, where I joined him. He hailed a taxi cab and we leaped in. Crewe gave the address that the operator had mentioned.

'Now, Langton,' he said as we leaned back, 'the question is whether Randall will present that check for payment first, or whether, as is more probable, he'll go straight to his confederates. Undoubtedly all their plans are laid for a quick getaway. If he should go first to the bank, we shall still be in time to apprehend the others, and undoubtedly we can summon Randall to meet us by extracting from them the password, or whatever sign they have agreed upon.'

He called to the driver to make more speed and we drove through the slush, sending it flying in a muddy cloud on either side of us. Soon we had left the business section behind us and were speeding up Lexington Avenue. The park appeared; we passed it and approached the Harlem district.

'Are you armed?' I asked.

Crewe shook his head. 'It won't be necessary,' he answered. 'When I spoke of confederates, Langton, I should have used the singular. As a matter of fact, Randall has only one confederate — an elderly man, and somewhat infirm. The shock of our appearance will be sufficient to disarm the pair of them.'

At last we turned into Wilcox Avenue. No. 246 was a small tobacconist's shop with a pool room at the back, in which a number of ill-favored persons were playing upon a half-dozen tables. Crewe looked around him in some dismay.

'He's trickier than I thought,' he said. 'This place is only a way-station.'

'Want a game, gentlemen?' asked the proprietor, coming forward with an ill-smelling cigar between his lips.

'I want a word with you,' said Crewe, pulling him to one side. He looked through into the pool room; all the players were engaged and it seemed unlikely that we would be disturbed for a few minutes at least. Crewe took the fellow by the lapels of his coat.

'Did you convey that message to the old gentleman?' he asked.

The fellow started, but instantly regained his composure. 'What old gentleman?' he asked.

'None of that,' said Crewe. 'Things have gone wrong. Our friend can't be here. Is everything packed?'

The man hesitated and looked around shiftily. 'I can't talk to you until Mr. Somers arrives,' he said.

'Mr. Somers will *not* arrive,' cried Crewe in exasperation. 'Do you want to queer the whole game? Will you give him a telephone message from me?'

'What is it?' demanded the fellow sourly.

'Tell him to take a taxi and meet us at the Grand Central, in the smoking room. Mr. Somers will be there. Stop! I must use your telephone a moment.'

He went to the instrument and made as if to take down the receiver, then checked himself.

'See here, mister,' said the fellow, 'I don't know you, and I've got my orders strict. Now if I send your message, will you step outside the store so that you won't overhear the number?'

'That sounds good enough,' said Crewe. He took me by the arm and we went out of the shop, the proprietor watching us suspiciously until we had stepped across the threshold.

'Now, Langton,' said Crewe, 'he will undoubtedly call up the confederate, if only to voice suspicion of us. 'Quick! In here.'

He thrust me into a store three numbers away, outside which was the sign 'Local and Long Distance Telephone.' He hurried to the instrument and took down the receiver.

'Hello! Hello!' he called. 'This is for police headquarters. A call had just been taken from 8214 Harlem. I want the number.'

He waited one moment until the answer came, then seized me by the arm. 'We shall be just in time,' he said. 'It's a furnished room house on One Hundred and Fifty-Third Street.'

It was only twelve blocks distant and a short turn around the block. We were panting and breathless when we arrived at a dingy house with a sign saying 'Furnished Rooms' in a dirty window behind which bloomed a faded rubber plant.

'Have you any rooms?' asked Crewe. 'My friend and I are transients; we want a good-sized apartment for a few days. The cost is immaterial.'

The woman wiped her hands upon a dirty apron and looked at us suspiciously. 'I'll have the front parlor on the second floor vacant this afternoon,' she said. 'If you'd step up, maybe the gentleman would let you see it.'

She turned and we prepared to follow

her, when suddenly a taxi cab stopped in front of the house and a man dashed out at full speed and was up the stairs with a bound. He was breathing heavily, and his face was ash-gray as he espied us. We recognized him immediately, in spite of a pair of heavy spectacles and a newly shaven upper lip. It was Randall, the English secretary.

'Don't let them in,' he shrieked, and precipitated himself upon us with such fury that we all three fell to the floor while the landlady screamed and waved her arms over us in a strange sort of benediction.

'It's no use, Randall,' said Crewe. 'The game's up. Better come upstairs quietly.'

'Take that, curse you,' screamed the secretary, and snapped a revolver in his face. By some miracle the ball failed to reach its destination; it buried itself in the woodwork of the door. Next moment we had disarmed and trussed the man. He confronted us malignantly, his face like putty, the breath hooting from between his lips.

'Come, Randall,' said Crewe quietly. 'It

could have been far worse than it is, you know. It could have been *murder*.'

'I wish to God it were,' snapped the Englishman vindictively.

'Now suppose you go ahead, and we'll follow you,' said Crewe, pressing the revolver into the small of Randall's back. 'Now, madam, will you kindly give your lungs a breathing space? It's no use calling 'police,' for we represent the central office.'

Randall sullenly proceeded up the stairs, and we followed. At the top of the first flight he stopped in front of the parlor. 'Silly old fool. I told him to keep his eyes peeled,' he muttered. 'Walk in, gentlemen,' he continued, standing aside.

'After you,' said Crewe, pushing him into the room. We followed into a plainly furnished apartment containing a large bed, three chairs and a writing table. Several pieces of English baggage were upon the floor, packed ready for departure. Seated at the window, looking toward us with a heavy face of mingled fear and doubt, was an elderly gentleman whose expression seemed familiar to me, though I could not recall where I had seen him before.

Crewe stepped forward with a laugh and took the heavy face between his hands. Next moment he stepped back. In either hand was a false blue-black whisker, which he had peeled from the skin.

'Langton,' he said mockingly, 'allow me to present to you our esteemed friend, Sir Moresby Blount.'

The expression upon the financier's face was comical to witness. All his dignity had deserted him, and he leaned back in the chair breathing stertorously, apparently in acute and craven fear.

'We nearly missed you, Randall,' said Crewe, turning to the secretary. 'Tell me one thing. Have you presented the check for payment?'

'No,' Randall growled. 'That was to have been the last thing done.'

'I thought so,' answered Crewe. 'Payment has been stopped. You would have been arrested at the bank. We had you either way.'

'Well, what are you going to do?' asked Randall, biting his lips nervously.

The answer was supplied by the unceremonious bursting open of the door. A couple of policemen stood upon the threshold; and, behind them, peering over their shoulders alternately, was the face of the landlady.

'I think we can fight the matter out at the police station,' Crewe answered.

The trial of Blount and Randall was, of course, one of the *causes célèbres* of the year. Having recovered the amount of its insurance, the Salamander Company decided not to put itself to the expense of a prosecution, since in any event the first claim upon the prisoners would have been that of the federal government. The Arizona development scheme proved to be a gigantic swindle. Blount was placed upon trial and sentenced to serve seven years in the federal prison at Atlanta, Georgia, while Randall, his tool, escaped with a sentence of three years.

It was disclosed at the trial that Blount had been implicated in a similar series of shady transactions in England. The crash of the Arizona scheme was followed by the collapse of seven of his banks in

London and the provinces. If the English government presses for his extradition when he is set free by the American government, doubtless a further sentence will befall him.

It appears that, rendered desperate by the impending crash of his fortunes, Blount had conceived the desperate scheme of feigning death in order to obtain the insurance money and start life anew in some other corner of the globe. The plan had been laid skillfully; the journey to America, where there was none to identify him positively, was a plot of genius. By arrangement a body had been removed from an undertaker's, mutilated and dressed in the financier's clothes, while he went into hiding until the Salamander Company should pay the insurance.

'But what gave you the idea that he was alive?' I asked of Crewe. 'How could you discover that the body wasn't Sir Moresby's, when the features were mutilated?'

Crewe smiled. 'It's so simple that I really hate to give the trick away,' he said.

'Perhaps you recollect the stained glove in my apartment?'

'Yes, and I wondered what on earth your object could be in dyeing it purple.'

'The purple was a simple coal tar dye, used extensively for hardening and bringing out the salient forms of microscopic subjects,' Crewe answered. 'I knew the moment I had it in my hands that the body at the morgue could *not* be Sir Moresby's. The ridges on the thumbs and fingers were what are technically known as 'whorls.' The ridges on Sir Moresby's fingers, on the other hand, were elliptical. They'd been well imprinted into the soft kid, and it was necessary only to turn the glove inside out and dye it in order to bring them out in marked detail.'

4

The Champion of the Fleet

In spite of an acquaintance which had lasted several months, I had never known that Peter Crewe was an Englishman. His accent was of that indeterminate character common to the educated class of both America and England, and I had learned very little about his antecedents, since he appeared to be wholly absorbed in his hobby of unraveling mysteries through the medium of his peculiar optical gift. That he had any interests outside this line of occupation was borne in upon me for the first time when going to his office to consult him relative to a client of mine. I found him reading a morning newspaper and giving vent to short and emphatic exclamations.

'Did you see this?' he cried. 'The American fleet's middleweight champion is to box our middleweight champion at

Coney Island tomorrow evening at eight.'

'*Our* champion?' I exclaimed.

'The champion of the visiting British fleet,' Crewe explained; and then I learned his nationality for the first time.

'Are you interested in boxing?' I asked in some surprise.

'I was a pupil of John L. Sullivan,' he answered proudly.

It developed that Crewe had been widely known at one time as a successful amateur boxer, and was still held in respect as a man of parts and a stickler for all the best traditions of the ring.

'It's strange that you should have brought up this subject,' I said, 'because it's about this very man — Thompson, the American middleweight — that I've come to consult you.'

'What's the trouble?' asked Crewe, laying his newspaper aside.

'I have an appointment with him at three,' I answered. 'Suppose you come over to my office and let him tell you his own story.'

Crewe agreed, and, promptly at the hour set, Thompson made his appearance. He was a handsome, well-set-up fellow, a seaman from the *North Dakota*, and a man of evident intelligence.

'Sit down, Thompson,' I said. Thompson complied, laying down his head-covering upon the table. 'Now,' I said, 'tell your story in detail.'

'Well, it's this way, Mr. Langton,' said Thompson, pulling up his trouser legs. 'Next week I shall be twenty-one, and if I live to reach my majority I inherit a snug little sum of fifty thousand dollars from the estate of my uncle in Ireland. If I don't live that long it goes to a distant connection of my uncle known as Philip Egan. It wasn't willed that way exactly, but there was a court case, and the lawyers fixed it that way between them after eating up half the estate in litigation; the sum left was nearly a hundred thousand.'

'And you've experienced some remarkable things during the past few days,' I continued.

'Yes, sir, as I told you this morning. We came ashore last week after a year's cruise, during which I hardly ever left the ship. Phil Egan was one of the first men I met on landing. He came up to me and shook hands. 'Frank,' he said, 'of course I hoped you wouldn't live long enough to get that money, but we're not going to let a little thing like that stand between friends, are we?' And though I've always mistrusted Phil, what could I do but give him the glad grip? So we saw the sights of the town together.

'Now sir, that was five days ago, and of course I've been careful of myself, being in training and having every hope of whipping the Britisher at the island tomorrow. And yet, it has seemed to me that my life wasn't in particularly good standing.

'That same night, while Phil and I were strolling down the Bowery, perfectly sober, we were attacked by a gang without a moment's warning. Phil got away; I knocked down two of them, and the third nearly got home with his knife on me.' He pulled down his sailor's collar and displayed a faint red scratch almost encircling his throat. 'That would have been a bad wound if it had gone an inch deeper, Mr. Langton,' he remarked philosophically. 'And the day before yesterday, when I was passing down a side street, I heard a snap at my side and a crack at a window opposite. I looked, and in the woodwork of a door behind me I found this, just embedded.' He took from his kerchief a .45-carbine bullet.

'You suspect Egan is trying to murder you for the sake of the money?' I asked.

'It wouldn't become me to say that, sir,' replied Thompson, 'although I haven't seen him since we were set upon by the gang. But if he's going to get me, he'll have to do it quickly, for I come of age on Saturday.'

'Did you go anywhere else with Egan?' Crewe asked.

'We took a turn round Coney Island a couple hours before we were attacked on the Bowery, sir,' Thompson answered.

'Now think. Did you do anything unusual at Coney?'

'Why, yes, sir,' answered Thompson, reddening. 'But it seems such a trifle, hardly worth mentioning.'

'Never mind. Out with it.'

'Well, the fact is, I got tattooed,' said Thompson. 'I'd always wanted to be done, and yet somehow I'd been a little shy; but Egan persuaded me, and I had an eagle put on my chest. Very artistically, too.'

'Let me see it,' said Crewe.

Thompson stripped, and a moment later we perceived the outlines of my national bird upon the sailor's chest. 'It's hardly sore at all,' said Thompson.

'And Egan persuaded you to have that done,' said Crewe thoughtfully. 'Now, have you a photograph of this man Egan?'

'Yes, sir, I brought it with me at Mr. Langton's instructions,' said the sailor. 'We were took together at Coney.'

Crewe took the photograph in his hand and focused his eyes upon it. 'Hm! These cheap photographs have one advantage over the expensive ones,' he said. 'They are truer to life; the photographers don't go in for retouching. Thank you, my friend,' he said, returning it. 'Now, let me give you one piece of advice. Go back to your ship and stay aboard her; don't leave until you come of age.'

'But the fight's tomorrow,' said Thompson helplessly.

75

'Miss it.'

'Why, sir, if I say it myself, I'm the only man in the fleet that can whip the Britisher. They've been bragging how they're going to put it all over us.'

'If you take part in that fight your chances of inheriting that money will be remote. Miss it, Thompson, and, whatever you do, wear a pad of soft cotton batting over that tattoo mark.'

The sailor rose with an expression of offended dignity. 'If that's all you can advise me, gentlemen,' he said, 'I must say my visit here hasn't done me much good.'

'It has saved you a lot of harm, young man,' said Crewe. 'At least you've had your warning. You don't intend to obey my suggestions, I suppose?'

'No, sir,' answered the sailor doggedly.

'Then that's all I have to say to you. No, Mr. Langton doesn't want to add anything. Good afternoon to you.' And he showed him out of the door.

'I must say, Crewe,' I began, 'you have a rather unceremonious manner of dismissing my clients.'

'Forgive me, Langton,' said Crewe, all penitence in a moment, 'but really I saw so much further ahead than you. I have reason to believe that a diabolical scheme has been put into execution which will result in the young man's death at the fight. Tell me, did you draw any deductions from the appearance or facts of the tattooing?'

'It looked a little bluer than the average tattoo mark,' I said.

'Excellent. Then you are beginning to observe,' said Crewe. 'But still, even if you could see all, that would help you little without a knowledge of that man Egan.'

'You've seen him before?' I asked.

'Several times. In the month of July, 1907, I saw him in the central criminal court, during the trial of three Chinese gunmen, when I happened in with a communication for the district attorney. I was at that time practicing law. The gun men were acquitted. A month later, while conducting a party of ladies over Chinatown, I saw him seated at a table with two of the same men, eating with chopsticks.'

'Now I see your point,' I exclaimed. 'The tattooing substance was of a poisonous nature, and — '

'In such a case I should hardly have permitted our friend to depart.'

'But surely you don't think that the English champion has been bribed to injure him?'

'No,' said Crewe, smiling. 'Still, at all hazards Thompson must not be allowed to participate in the boxing affray at Coney Island tomorrow. By the way, you don't know Chinese, I suppose?'

'No.'

'I often wish I did. With my power of visual retention, I'm able to reproduce practically every sign of the ten thousand commonly used in the Chinese written language. But unfortunately my memory is rather subnormal than extraordinary, and I'm never able to recollect what any of these signs mean. However, we have a little work to do in Chinatown.'

We took the Third Avenue elevated to that swarming region, walked up Mott Street, and halted before an obscure, dingy-looking shop in whose doorway stood a wide-hatted, felt-shoed Celestial.

'This,' said Crewe, 'is the headquarters of the Hip Sings, by which clan the gunmen I referred to were employed. What do you see in the window?'

I saw a miscellaneous assortment of firecrackers, preserves, vegetables, lacquer work, wood carvings, and kimonos.

'Now which of those Chinese labels should you say meant firecrackers, Langton?' asked my companion.

'That one,' I answered. 'Above those bunches of rockets.'

'I think so too. Now fix that sign in your mind. Our next objective is Coney Island.'

It was evening before we arrived, and the shows were in full swing. For miles the great white way stretched out before our eyes, glittering with electric lights, a veritable fairyland of fantasy. Half of New York seemed to have turned out to greet us, as well as all the sailors of both fleets, who were fraternizing and spending their shore money at the alluring sideshows. The whir of the scenic railroads, the shouts and laughter, and the popping at rifle booths made up that perfect pandemonium of sounds that can hardly be heard anywhere but at this national pleasure city.

'Now, Langton, we have to find our man,' said Crewe. 'I'm afraid that it's rather like searching for a needle in the proverbial haystack. Keep a sharp lookout for a Chinese tattooist, and we'll take in each alley in rotation.'

We traversed Coney Island and its purlieus for an hour and more without success. The booths, closely packed together, almost defied examination. One came upon them unexpectedly in corners, and one stumbled round alleys upon the same streets that one had just quitted; our chance of singling out this particular booth seemed almost impossibly remote.

Suddenly Crewe gripped my arm. 'You know that man?' he asked, pointing to a flashily dressed fellow who slunk along with a peculiarly sinister gait in front of us.

'No,' I replied.

'That's Egan,' he answered. 'Disguised, but he couldn't take out that wrinkle about the eyebrow. Now, let's tail him.'

We followed him for five minutes or more; then he turned aside abruptly and came to a halt in front of a Japanese rice-cake booth, in a corner of which we now perceived a savage-looking ruffian seated, apparently aimlessly staring out upon the crowds. At either side was a small stock of Chinese goods, which, however, he was making no attempt to sell.

'You recognize the firecracker symbol?' asked Crewe.

I did not recognize it, and should never have remembered those apparently meaningless hieroglyphics. Crewe, however, seemed to be in high spirits.

'Now a great deal hinges upon one thing,' he said. 'It's my belief that Thompson didn't tell us his whole story. In other words, I believe that he's been induced to return for a final treatment either tonight or tomorrow.'

'Surely not immediately before the fight,' I suggested.

'Most persons have no common sense about themselves. Ten to one he'll be here. The only thing to do is wait for him.'

There was a conveniently secluded place across the alley. Since neither of us was known to Egan, it was arranged that we should take our seats within this beer garden and remain there, ordering drinks at intervals in as great a quantity as might be necessary to prevent our ejection by the management.

'Langton,' said Crewe when we were seated with our full glasses before us, 'I'm more certain than ever that a most ingenious and diabolical plot has been hatched for that young seaman's death, and that in return for services rendered him by Egan, that Chinese criminal has consented to cooperate with him. The sight of the firecrackers has confirmed me in this belief. And if Thompson meets the English champion, his death will be a foregone conclusion.'

'But could they not kill him without such a meeting?' I asked.

'They could, undoubtedly. A fistic encounter between Egan or some hired bully and Thompson would have the same result, so far as Thompson is concerned. But there'd be two drawbacks to such a plan. In the first place, the survivor would probably be arrested and have to stand his trial for manslaughter. In the second place, the encounter would not be without danger to the life of the other party. By making the Englishman the innocent participant in the murder, all danger is removed so far as concerns the conspirators.'

I was more piqued than ever, but I knew that it was not Crewe's custom to explain his theories until the denouement. I revolved a dozen ideas in my mind. My speculations were cut short by my perceiving Egan prepare to move away. In his farewell of the gunman there appeared to be a glance of perfect understanding.

'Follow him, Langton,' whispered Crewe. 'It isn't essential that we know where he's going, but it's desirable in case more mischief is brewing. Don't be more than fifteen minutes, though, in any event.'

I went in pursuit of Egan, who moved off furtively through the crowds. He made his way in the direction of the American camp, where the sailors of the English fleet were being regaled at a clambake by their American comrades. The affair was practically over; as I approached the canvas which had been set up I perceived a hilarious crowd composed of the crews of both nations, streaming out arm in arm, laughing and chattering together. Egan made his way toward a large gathering of men which seemed to form the nucleus of the mob.

Suddenly the crowd opened and I perceived Thompson struggling in the arms of a dozen sturdy compatriots, who, elated with the festive meal, insisted, apparently, in carrying him in state down the main avenue of Coney. He regained his feet at last and stood in their midst, flushed and a little unsteady. I was astonished to see that he had evidently been drinking, in spite of his training. At the same moment he perceived Egan.

'Hello, Phil,' he shouted, and shook the man by the hand warmly; then flung his arms around him. It was evident that prudence was no part of that particular sailor's nature. I reasoned that, angered by the unsatisfactory result of his interview with Crewe and myself that morning, he had experienced an entire revulsion of feeling. Doubtless Egan was now, to him, his best friend, and we were malingers and conspirators against his much-wronged relative. I wondered how much he would tell Egan; whether he would put him upon his guard.

The pair sauntered slowly along the avenue, despite the efforts of a fiery little man, apparently Thompson's trainer, who made wild endeavors to head him off. Thompson shook off the little man as though he were a fly, while his companions, evidently secure in their belief of the sailor's ability to dispose of the Englishman, trained or untrained, warmly seconded their mate. The little man gave up at last and, after shaking his fist angrily in Thompson's face, disappeared among the crowds.

Thereupon Thompson and Egan, arm in arm, surrounded by a round dozen of their cronies, strolled slowly in the direction of the tattooist's booth.

I hastened after them, and, by making a detour, succeeded in getting ahead of them at the next block, and, in reaching the booth a couple of minutes ahead of the party. I hurried across the alley to where I had left Crewe at the beer garden table.

Where was Crewe? Could that be he, that rough looking man, collarless, with dirty reversible cuffs and open waistcoat, his face flushed with drink, who was inviting all and sundry to come and sit down and drink at his expense? Undoubtedly it was Crewe, on closer inspection, for I had seen him in that same disguise upon a previous occasion; but I was certain that the sailor would never recognize him for the immaculate counselor of the afternoon.

Crewe was acting his part to the life. To the keenest observer he would have appeared nothing more than some flash bully who, having pulled off a haul somehow, was spending it in the only way he knew and acting the 'good fellow' to his improvised cronies.

'Here! *Garçon!* — Waiter!' he yelled. 'Bring us a quart bottle of fizzy drink. And say, you see that the ice's cold, or I'll knock your block off.' And he flung down a fifty dollar bill upon the beer-soaked table, which the waiter ran to seize with avidity.

As I lingered near, Crewe's sharp eye was turned on me.

'Come here, boy,' he yelled. 'Have a drink. Gentlemen, a friend. My friend — gentlemen,' he added in introduction; and, rather disgusted with the part we were to play, I sat down at an adjoining table, which was already filled with Crewe's strange guests.

None of them addressed me, however, being all apparently bent upon the possibility of extracting some money or drinks from Crewe.

Then the uproarious crowd of sailors turned into the alley and lined up in front of the booth. I heard Egan's voice ring out, apparently to smother some protest.

'Shut your face,' he yelled to the objector. 'Let him be vaccinated if he wants to be. Show 'em your chest, Frank. Look, boys. Ain't that the finest eagle you've ever seen! That's the Yankee eagle,' he continued, 'and I don't want anybody to tell me that Frank can't beat the

Britisher with that eagle on his chest. If anybody tells me so,' he continued, looking around, 'let him step up and say so, and I'll smash his face in.'

Either nobody disagreed with the speaker's views, or else each of the sailors felt that his face would be more suitable if it were not smashed in. With a look of triumph Egan turned to the tattooist and pushed Thompson into a chair. The tattooist took out his needles and pigments and began his work.

There is some psychological moment when the noisiest crowd becomes momentarily silent. At such a time the voice of some individual will arise and dominate the mob. So, at this juncture, the drunken tones of Crewe came floating across the still air.

'*To hell with the American eagle!*'

A dozen sailors sprang round, glaring. 'What's that? *What's that?*' they cried. 'Who *said* that?'

'*I* said that,' shouted Crewe, rising and swaggering unsteadily toward them. 'To *hell* with the American eagle,' he repeated with drunken gravity. 'There's no Yank living but a little Canadian can knock the five-spot off every time.'

There was a rush in Crewe's direction. In an instant he was surrounded by a mob of excited seamen, while his new friends made themselves scarce, evidently unwilling to share his unpopularity, yet not *wholly* absenting themselves, in case of further profits to come.

'You'll take that back,' shouted a brawny sailorman, shaking his fist under Crewe's nose. 'You'll eat them words or I'll make squash pie out of you.'

'You will, will you?' replied Crewe sneeringly. 'Twelve to one — twelve Yanks to one Canadian, and that's about your measure. There ain't a man here I can't lick singly in fair fight.'

Crewe had forced his way to Thompson's side. The sailor had just been released from the tattooist's charge and was rearranging his clothes. Now, hearing these words, he sprang up glaring.

'Let me get at him,' he shouted.

'No, no, Frank don't fight. You got to save your hands for tomorrow, Frank,' cried his supporters.

'Let him fight,' shouted Egan. 'What's the odds? It won't take many seconds to put that slob out of business. Say, do you mean what you said?' he yelled, thrusting his face within an inch of Crewe's.

'I surely do, and here's to prove it,' Crewe answered, and his fist shot out and caught Egan on the point of the jaw. I saw the man collapse, crumple up, and lie still. It was one of the cleanest fighting blows I had ever seen delivered.

Infuriated by the defeat of his relation, Thompson darted forward, his fists whirling like engine shafts. There was nothing of science shown. Crewe fought pluckily, but it was evident that he could not stand for long before those sledge-hammer blows. He sprang forward and the men clinched. I heard a short, quick snap, and heard the sailor utter an exclamation of pain. He fell back and looked down at his hands stupidly. One dangled limply from the wrist, as though it were broken.

With a yell the whole mob rushed upon Crewe. In an instant a free fight was in progress. Benches were torn up, tables seized; and, while the uproar was at its highest, each man vainly struggling to get at the supposed Canadian, Crewe calmly slipped away, just in time to escape the attentions of a body of police, who came charging with drawn clubs.

'It was a foul blow, Langton,' said Crewe to me on the following day. 'But unquestionably it was justified for the saving of the man's life. By the way, I see that the Englishman *easily* defeated Thompson's substitute.'

'What was the substance used by the tattooist?' I asked, ignoring Crewe's snide aside, and knowing that Crewe's story would *have* to be drawn out of him piecemeal.

'One of the iodides,' he answered, 'and the most powerful explosives known. So violent are they in their action that, if a few grains be strewn upon the face of a watch, the hands, coming in contact with them, will detonate them and blow the whole watch to pieces.'

'How did you come to suspect that this substance had been used, and how was it intended to work?'

'Do you know what they used to rub into soldier's wounds in olden days, Langton?' my companion asked.

I shook my head.

'*Gunpowder*. The explosives have the property of being very well tolerated by the tissues of the human body. Thompson's statement that the tattooing caused barely any irritation, the peculiarly blue appearance of the scar, and the relationship existing between Egan and the tattooist, who was connected with a firm of firecracker importers, all confirmed me in my suspicion. The plan was, undoubtedly, to let Thompson meet the Englishman. The first hard blow that he received upon the chest would certainly have detonated the explosive and blown out the vital organs of the body, producing instant death.

'You know that, when a foreign substance enters the tissues, nature, unable to reject it, renders it harmless by encysting it. It was the fear that this encysting process might already have begun which caused Egan to insist upon a second application.

'If the substance could have been removed, I would have confided in Thompson. But any attempt to cut out the explosive would have caused an immediate detonation. My problem, therefore, was to prevent the fight by rendering Thompson powerless without striking him upon the chest, as Egan hoped I would when he incited him to attack me. And but for that,' concluded Crewe, with a touch of pride in his tones, 'I think I *could* have given a better account of myself in our little tussle.'

'I suppose there is no chance of bringing the criminals to justice,' I suggested. 'Thompson would be the first to take the part of Egan. At least he ought to know the truth.'

'What for?' asked Crewe. 'He will be well protected in the ship's hospital, the explosive will have become encysted within a few days, and Thompson will certainly inherit that legacy. Langton,' he said, looking at me whimsically, 'you, as a lawyer, ought to know that the wise man is he who knows when to keep his mouth shut.'

5

The Record on the Screen

The case against Sanford certainly looked bleak enough. He had been arrested upon the charge of having murdered his wife, and the evidence against him was as follows:

His wife, a vaudeville actress, had left him the preceding spring and had refused to return to him. The principal cause for this separation appeared to have been his inability to support her in comfort, so that she preferred independence, with the certainty of a moderate income through her own efforts, to the tiresome routine of household duties in the home of a man earning a clerk's salary. During the unseasonable months of July and August she had earned a livelihood by posing for moving picture plays. Sanford had repeatedly visited her at her apartment to beseech her to return to him. He had been heard to utter threats in case she remained obdurate. On the occasion of his last visit previous to the tragedy his wife had been heard to order him out of the house, and she had forbidden him to molest her further.

One week later, at nine o'clock in the morning, the maid who came in daily to clean the apartment found Mrs. Sanford lying dead in a chair with a deep stab wound immediately beneath the right arm. Death had evidently been almost instantaneous, for there was no sign of a struggle, and the woman's face was as tranquil as though she had flung herself down upon the cushions for a brief rest after the labors of the day.

The chief witness against Sanford was the woman who rented the apartment adjacent to Mrs. Sanford's. She testified that she had met Sanford upon the stairs on the preceding evening, had seen him enter his wife's apartment, and subsequently heard the sounds of a violent altercation, after which Sanford left the house in a condition of intense excitement. Two hours or so later she heard him return and ring

Mrs. Sanford's bell. She heard voices raised in altercation in the apartment and heard Sanford again leave, but in a stealthy and secretive manner wholly unlike his usual method of departure. She heard him creep down the stairs and listened at the wall, but could make out no further sound next door. Doubtless the murder had already been accomplished.

The weapon with which the murder had been committed was found in a contiguous building lot next day. It was a Malay Kris, a knife with an incredibly keen edge, which Mrs. Sanford had owned, and the murder had been committed with an upward thrust. Upon the right side of the ivory handle, when the blade was held edge upward, were the blood-prints of four gloved fingers.

When called in for the defense I urged Sanford to plead guilty to manslaughter. I told him there was every reason to hope that he would escape with a sentence of fifteen or twenty years. In the first place, the fact that he had worn gloves, in the second the fact that the weapon had been taken from Mrs. Sanford's wall, where it had hung, clearly indicated absence of premeditation. The jury would show every consideration to a man whose wife had deserted him. But Sanford obstinately insisted that he was innocent. He admitted that he had called on Mrs. Sanford the evening before the tragedy to induce her to return to him. She had refused, he said, and taunted him with the story of a rival for whose sake she intended to obtain a divorce.

I was only half convinced, in spite of the vehemence of Sanford's denial. I have heard criminals assert their innocence most convincingly, only to admit their guilt after conviction.

'Have you any theory as to who the murderer was?' I asked.

'The man she taunted me about,' cried Sanford. 'He had been pestering her for weeks to divorce me and marry him, had threatened her with death unless she consented. She pretended to me that she intended to comply; but I know in my heart that she always loved me. If I had only earned more money she would have come back to me. Do you think I should have hung round her for months without some reasonable hope? I tell you she hated that fellow; she just tried to play each of us off against the other.'

Sanford insisted that this man had been the second visitor on the night of the murder, and had slain Mrs. Sanford in a jealous rage when she finally refused to marry him. But he had never seen him and knew nothing of his identity.

That was all I had to go upon. The woman in the apartment next to Mrs. Sanford's admitted that she had not actually seen Sanford return on the night of the murder. She was convinced, however, that the second visitor was he. She had no reason for this conviction, but she was all the more certain of it.

I was willing to believe that Sanford had had a rival for Mrs. Sanford's affections, and that he had frequently visited the woman. Probably she had been holding off both men until she could decide to which one it would prove more profitable to attach herself. In fact, Mrs. Sanford had had frequent visitors; she was an attractive woman, and it was not hard to believe that some of them must have fallen in love with her. But that any of these had murdered her seemed quite unlikely. The particular rival of whom Sanford spoke was quite unknown to Mrs. Sanford's acquaintances; if such as one existed, his identity had been skillfully concealed. To discover him seemed an impossibility. There was no letter, no shred of evidence, pointing to such a man.

In my perplexity, I arranged to bring in Peter Crewe. 'Let us begin by assuming that such a man exists,' said Crewe, when he had heard my story attentively. 'Are there any photographs of men in Mrs. Sanford's apartment?'

There were dozens of photographs of both men and women. In fact Mrs. Sanford had had a hobby for collecting photographs of all her acquaintances. The apartment had been sealed by the police, but, upon obtaining an order from the authorities, we were enabled to enter. We found photographs all around the sitting room.

'If it is one of these,' I said, 'nobody knows which one.'

'That is immaterial, so long as it *is* one of them,' said Crewe, focusing his eyes upon each in turn. He remained thus for several seconds in front of each photograph, as though some time were needed for the action of the light to impress the images indelibly upon the retina.

'Now,' said Crewe, 'the probabilities are that she met him in the moving picture company for which she posed. Actresses and actors generally form a close corporation, and we may almost take it for granted that they belonged to the same trade. By the way, Langton, the photograph we are looking for is probably not here.'

'*Not* here?' I exclaimed.

'No,' he said, pointing to the velvet mantel cover. 'Do you see anything strange there? Surely you must, for it is impossible to keep a secret from velvet.'

'I see some dust,' I said.

'Look *here* — and *here* — and *here*,' said Crewe impatiently. 'Do you see that faint line along the nap of the velvet? That is where a photograph stood for several weeks, but stands no longer. Observe that there is an edging of dust on either side of it. And here, and here, these photographs beside it once stood, but they were recently moved up about an inch and a half closer. Langton, the murderer undoubtedly took away his photograph and moved up the photographs on either side in order to cover the gap left by the removal. It was ingenious, and would have baffled the police. But velvet tells its own tale, and all the rubbing in the world would not have erased those creases in the nap. We are, then, bent upon the search for a man whose photograph is *not* here — Mrs. Sanford's only friend whom we have not seen. It simplifies matters enormously!'

'How?' I asked.

'In the first place it bears out your theory as to the existence of such a man, whom we have hitherto only assumed to exist. Secondly, we know all Mrs. Sanford's friends but him. Consequently, when we see him in the moving pictures we know him instantly. But it is essential, in order to verify certain suspicions that I entertain, that we should see the knife.'

'That can be done,' I said. 'It is in the custody of the police, but I have the right to inspection. Let us go round to police headquarters immediately.'

No demur was made to our examining the weapon, although a detective remained at hand while we looked at it. It was a formidable affair, and one which had evidently been put to use by its Malay owner before it crossed the seas to become the property of the luckless actress. Its blade curled in a succession of waves, and it was as keen as the finest razor. Upon the right side, when held blade upward, appeared the bloody glove-prints.

'If them was only fingerprints, now,' said the detective, 'we'd know who done it instantly. Fingers are never the same, but gloves baffles us.'

'On the contrary,' said Crewe, 'I think we shall run the murderer to earth with equal facility.'

'You've got him, that's why,' said the detective, chuckling. 'Gents, it's as clean a case against the accused as we've handled this year.'

'Not if he knows how to pitch quoits,' said Crewe, sharply.

'What's that you say?' asked the detective.

'I said, 'not if he knows how to pitch quoits,'' said Crewe. 'Come, Langton, this is a very important point. We must stop in at a sporting shop and get some quoits. I suppose the prisoner will be allowed to pitch them in the prison yard?'

I was lost in amazement at this new scheme of Crewe's, but I knew that it was useless to ask for an explanation until the unfolding of the plot. We purchased a half dozen quoits and took them to our prisoner, to whom I introduced my companion. Sanford was inclined to be sullen at first, and demurred when requested to pitch the quoits.

'Sanford,' I whispered, 'there's more in this than you or I know. Don't be obstinate. Mr. Crewe has got men out of worse troubles, and apparently by just such aimless means.'

'You can't hand him those things, gentlemen,' said the jailer, 'without a special order. I'm sorry, but that's the strict rule.'

'Well, then,' said Crewe, 'let me see you pitch them in imagination. Now, here is the board. You have a quoit in your hand. Now heave it.'

Sanford complied in a reluctant manner. Though his action was not very graphic, it evidently satisfied Crewe.

'Excellent, Langton,' he commented. 'I have learned all that it was necessary to know. And now we have to find Mrs. Sanford's friend whose photograph was removed from the mantel.'

'And that,' I said, 'is the beginning of the whole difficulty. We seem to be no nearer that than at the first.'

'If we can find the identity of the man,' said Crewe, 'the rest will be easy. Now the probabilities are strongly in favor of his having acted in the same company with her. In such event we shall find him upon the screen at some moving picture show.'

'But,' I interpolated, 'how will you know it *is* the man? Will you suspect every actor whose photograph was not among Mrs. Sanford's effects? It seems to me you are stretching your point very far. I confess I do not know what your clue is.'

'Patience, Langton,' said Crewe, smiling. 'If I were to tell you I should cease to be a mystery and become a very ordinary mortal in your eyes. I confess that I enjoy the role of the enigma.'

The company for which Mrs. Sanford had posed was at this time advertising a new play daily. It controlled some three or four dozen moving picture theaters in town, and as the plays grew stale they were sent out into the county districts. To find the man we were seeking, it would therefore be necessary to make a careful and methodical investigation of all the theaters which this company controlled. We spent nearly a week of nights in our search before we found what we were looking for.

It was at a little cheap theater in a slum that had grown up among a maze of shops that catered to the needs of the residents in a new district of high flats and ostentatious, if overblown, wealth. The play was a typical southern drama. In a cell crouched a disheveled man, arrested upon a charge of murder. Outside collected the mob, infuriated with liquor, thirsting for the prisoner's blood. With ropes and pistols in their hands they demanded that the sheriff bring out his prisoner.

Then the sheriff's daughter came out to

persuade the crowd to abandon its intentions. As the girl tripped forward across the screen Crewe and I recognized Mrs. Sanford.

Awed for an instant, the mob quickly regained its courage. It demanded that the sheriff come out in person. Among the leaders of the crowd I recognized several of the originals of Mrs. Sanford's photographs. Evidently Crewe's theory was correct — that she selected her friends from among her own profession.

Suddenly the jail doors flew open and the sheriff came out in person. He strode forward, tall, scowling, menacing. In one hand he held a revolver, and, as he came to a stop, he pointed this at the breast of the mob leader.

'There is our murderer,' Crewe whispered to me, in the moment of tense interest and silence that followed the denouement.

The scene ended and a long-drawn sigh went up from the audience in the little theater. Single-handed, the sheriff had defied the crowd; with his menacing revolver he had driven them from the jail precincts. What next? The interval was long and tantalizing, and every shadowy profile in the audience seemed to disclose a mouth that gaped for some sensational climax.

'That is our man,' repeated Crewe with sure conviction.

I was conscious of a sensation of rising anger. It angered me to be made the butt of his fantasies, to sit beside him and hear him calmly announce his conclusions while my mind was striving painfully to pass from one inference to the next.

'Well, I won't dispute your statement,' I rejoined. 'But even if it is — I see no reason why it should be, but even if it is — how are you going to locate him? His photograph may be doing stunts on the screen while the man in person is well on his way to Alaska or South America, or Timbuctoo.'

'They always come back,' said Crewe. 'Why, the first instinct of any murderer is flight.'

'Not in crimes of jealousy,' Crewe answered. 'And then there is the thrill of seeing an innocent man arrested and likely to suffer the penalty for the crime.

No, no, Langton, our friend is not very far from this city. I should not be surprised to come upon him any day, in the court, the street. Besides, you must remember that no photograph of him exists; he thinks he is secure.'

'And yet I'm willing to wager,' said I, 'that, granting your theories are true, which I do not for the moment admit, the original of that sheriff is not within a thousand miles of us at this moment.'

A new scene was thrown upon the screen. The gaping mouths opened wide; the audience settled down for its further installment of thrill. And then — I think my hair verily stood upon end — as if by some magnetic compulsion my eyes turned toward a man seated upon the end bench immediately across the aisle. There was the original of the sheriff in the play, seated with folded arms, but staring as if hypnotized at that phantasm of himself that strode and swore and played the hero by the side of the trembling daughter, while the mob menaced them, yet impotent before the revolver which he held in the crook of his strong right arm.

I turned to Crewe. I caught his arm. 'Look! *Look!*' I whispered, pointing.

For once my companion appeared to lose his self-possession. His eyes shifted alternately from the play-actor upon the screen to the man on the bench and back again.

'Langton,' he said, 'for once you get the better of me. Fool that I was, I was so absorbed in theorizing that *I* didn't *look*. I didn't dare to hope it might be true. Watch him and, when the act ends, we will take seats on either side of him. You sit on his left and keep your eyes on his hand — his *left* hand.'

We took our places accordingly as soon as the moving figures faded from the screen. The man never stirred as we sat down beside him. His gaze was fixed singly upon the screen, and he waited for the final act of the drama. All round us rose the excited hum of voices. Crewe touched our man upon the arm, and he started in his place and leaned toward him nervously.

'Keep quiet,' said Crewe in a warning voice. 'After this act I want you to come with me and explain about the murder of Mrs. Sanford.'

Quick as a flash the man's left hand went down toward his hip pocket. I caught it and compressed it firmly between my own.

'Well done, Langton,' said Crewe in a whisper. 'Now, sir, will you come quietly?'

A shiver ran through our captive's frame. He turned his eyes from one to another of us. Then he seemed to break down and he collapsed in his seat limply.

'I killed her,' he muttered. 'Do what you like with me. I meant to give myself up anyway. Every day I have haunted the district, hoping that I might be arrested, intending to confess, but I hadn't the nerve. I am glad it's over.'

'Will you come now?' said Crewe.

'Let me see the last act,' he pleaded. 'My God, you don't know what it means to realize that I shall never see her face again in life, except upon that screen. I've come here nightly to look at her. Let me wait till the end.'

'On one condition,' said Crewe. 'Langton, take his pistol out of his left hip pocket.'

'What I still fail to understand,' I said to Crewe, much later after he had been arrested and taken away, 'is how you came to associate this man with the murder. Even if his photograph were not among Mrs. Sanford's effects, still there must have been many of her acquaintances who were similarly absent. To me it all seems like a happy guess.'

'The only guess,' said Crewe, 'was in the assumption that the murderer had been an actor in the same company. And that was rather a probability than a fortunate hypothesis.'

'But what enabled you to feel so sure that you were able to charge the man directly with the commission of the crime?'

'Let's go back a way,' Crewe answered. 'The wound, if you remember, was immediately beneath the woman's right arm. The murder had been committed while she lay back in her chair.'

'Yes.'

'Did it occur to you that the murderer must have stood in a very cramped position to inflict the wound in such a location? And that it would be almost impossible to drive home the steel forcibly enough to cause immediate death?'

'I confess that it did not. The evidence against Sanford seemed so convincing.'

'When you saw the knife, did you deduce anything from the fact that the fingerprints were on the right side of the blade?'

'Where else would they be?'

'Take out your pocket-knife. Open it. Hold it edge upward. Now on which side are the fingerprints?'

'On the left side,' I said, much chagrined.

'Then the inference is — ?'

'That the murderer was left-handed.'

'Exactly; and this accounts for the position of the wound. If he held the weapon in his left hand the blow would fall most naturally where it did. Many people, Langton, are partly left-handed; that is to say, having been trained to the use of the right hand, they revert to their natural instinct in moments of excitement. Our murderer was doubtless one of this large class; therefore it is not necessary to suppose that he used his left hand habitually, in which event he would have left traces that would have aroused the attention even of the police. Well, then, when I went to the moving picture show I was looking for an unknown man with a left-handed instinct. Did you notice nothing in that scene with the mob?'

'He held his pistol in his left hand!' I exclaimed.

'Yes. But you saw it and let it slip through the gates of memory.'

'One more question. Why the quoits?'

'Merely to ascertain beyond a doubt that our friend Sanford was not left-handed himself,' chuckled Crewe.

6

A Matter of Mathematics

Of the many problems which were solved through the aid of Peter Crewe, I think the one that involved the capture of Rowell, the defaulting bank cashier, was the most remarkable. Crewe's skill rested in the main upon a certain optical gift by virtue of which he was enabled at any time to call up before his mental vision the picture of any person or thing that he had once inspected, and that complete and in every detail perfect. But while this faculty was largely instrumental in Rowell's capture, this case involved so clear and close a piece of mathematical reasoning that it deserves to be set down as one of the masterpieces of detective induction.

Crewe and I were in England upon some business at the time when the robbery of the Penny and Shilling Bank startled the country. Rowell, the cashier, had somehow managed to obtain possession of no less a sum than a hundred and sixty thousand pounds. He had quietly secreted this in his briefcase, walked out of the bank on Saturday at noon, and completely disappeared by the time the discovery of the theft was made on Monday.

Rowell had no relatives and no close friends. He had no ties, no acquaintances among the criminal class. He looked like many another young Englishman of the middle classes: of medium height, stalwart, alert, aggressive, clean. He left no photograph behind. There seemed to be no way in which he could be traced.

The superintendent of Scotland Yard made a happy suggestion to the bank manager. I had been called into consultation as the bank's attorney, and I had brought Crewe to the conference with me. We both strongly approved the plan.

'Every Englishman who's committed a felony makes the United States his ultimate objective,' the superintendent said. 'Why this should be so, I don't pretend to know. I don't mean to cast a slur upon your country. Still, the fact remains that when he thinks the hue and cry have died away, he takes ship for America.

'Now, the proposition is to herd him into what I'll call a rat trap. So long as he lies low in England, he's never likely to be discovered. But if we make the chase hot at every point except the western ports, and if we publish items in the newspapers stating that no guard is being kept at Liverpool or Southampton, because the fugitive is believed to be in France, he'll be tempted; he'll investigate to discover whether this is true. Finally, emboldened, he'll take ship for New York.'

'And then?' asked Crewe.

'We arrest him as he disembarks.'

This plan was carried out and worked to perfection. Although Rowell could not be positively identified, there was every reason to believe in a cable statement from the captain of the *Pentannic* to the effect that the fugitive had taken passage on his ship. The information was cabled back to New York and a couple of detectives were detailed to arrest Rowell the moment that he landed.

Unfortunately, the plan miscarried. As we learned afterward, Rowell had somehow possessed himself of the uniform of a ship's officer, and attired in this guise, had stepped boldly ashore under the noses of the detectives and disappeared among the four million inhabitants of the city.

The bank urged me to hasten to America in order to assist in the work of capture. I had, however, interested the manager in Crewe by recounting some of my companion's former successes, and at his invitation I brought my friend to the scene of the robbery.

'You say you have no photograph of the thief?' asked Crewe when he heard the details of the story.

'None whatever. And I fancy,' said the manager, 'that you won't get much of a clue by examining his stool and counter.'

'I hope you're mistaken,' answered Crewe, laughing. 'May I ask you a few questions?'

'With pleasure.'

'What was Rowell's salary?'

'Two hundred pounds,' answered the manager with some hesitancy. 'We intended to increase it on the first of the year.'

'Still, a single man could live well on that,' said Crewe. 'Did he dress well?'

'Not extravagantly, but neatly. He usually wore a suit of blue serge, a collar of moderate height, and a gray tie.'

'That is *very* important,' said Crewe. 'But here's a more important matter still. Has the height of this stool been changed since Rowell vacated it?'

'No. It is an immovable seat, as you'll see, and nicely apportioned to the height of the counter.'

'In that case,' said Crewe, 'I think that we shall catch your man. By the way, did he ever wear anything but blue serge?'

'Rarely. That was his office coat, and he also wore it upon the streets. As you know, Mr. Crewe, the habit of the silk and morning coat isn't insisted upon anymore by many places of business.'

'And — one more question — you've had an unusually sunny summer, I believe?'

'They say so,' answered the manager

suavely, but looking at me as though to ask, *Is the fellow a dangerous lunatic?*

Without further remark, Crewe seated himself upon the stool and leaned over the desk. The sunlight streamed through the grille in front of the desk and in upon Crewe. He adjusted his position until he was seated exactly in the center of the stool; then, after an instant's silence, as though he were lost in meditation, he slipped down to the ground.

'Good morning, Mr. Simpson,' he said, extending his hand to the bank manager. 'If we get to New York before the police capture him, I hope to have the pleasure of presenting Mr. Rowell to you. And that,' he added, 'is probable enough, since the police are dealing with an extremely astute gentleman.'

We made our way to New York and had an interview with the head of the police department. He informed me of the situation in regard to the missing man. That he was in the city was a certainty. Had any authentic portrait of him existed, he would undoubtedly have been captured long before. At present it seemed almost impossible to take him. But if Rowell was immune from arrest, he in turn could not leave New York. Detectives were watching every road, every flight, every railroad station, every ferry house from which boats left for the New Jersey shore. Rowell's only possible point of escape was Long Island. He could doubtless evade the detectives and cross the Brooklyn Bridge during the rush hour. But that would be a risky proceeding, for though Brooklyn lay open to him, he could not cross from any point of Long Island to the Connecticut shore, while his return to New York itself would be fraught with dangers. It was highly probable, therefore, that Rowell was still within the limits of the borough of Manhattan.

'Where are you searching?' Crewe asked the police chief.

'We have two dozen men looking through the whole city,' said the latter. 'We're raking it with a fine-toothed comb. Sooner or later he must be found.'

'The only drawback to that scheme is that while you're raking one district, Rowell is likely to be in another.'

'Well, how would you do better?' asked the police chief, nettled.

'Why,' said Crewe, 'search all districts simultaneously.'

'Let me tell you,' said the chief of police, 'that the number of detectives at my disposal for this case is twenty-four, not twenty-four thousand.'

'Nevertheless, if you'll place four of your two dozen at my disposal for a week, I'll guarantee to find Rowell if he's within the limits of Manhattan borough,' said Crewe. 'And the glory's yours,' he added.

'I'll say nothing to the newspapers,' I announced. 'You stand to win either way. Either you score off Crewe, or you get the credit for the capture.'

The police chief pressed a bell. 'Send Cohen, O'Rourke, Murphy and Kelly here at once,' he said to the messenger. Almost immediately, the four policemen came in and saluted.

'You will place yourselves under the orders of this gentleman,' said the chief, indicating Crewe. 'It's the Rowell case, and *he* thinks he can work on it better than I can.'

'Report to me here tomorrow morning at nine,' said Crewe. 'You may take the day off. I want to think. I suppose you're all proficient in simple arithmetic?' he added, without a trace of sarcasm. They nodded. 'I'm glad to hear it. You may have a little adding to do.'

I did not see Crewe again until the second afternoon, when we met by appointment and lunched together. After the meal I asked him how he was progressing with his case.

'I've got the town staked out,' Crewe answered, 'and I think that the fourth day will witness Mr. Rowell's arrest. Of course, I could take him earlier by haphazard means, but I prefer to use the scientific method.'

'Will you inform me how, with four detectives, you can possibly have 'staked out' the town, as you phrase it?' I asked, a little exasperated.

'It's a matter of pure mathematics, Langton,' Crewe answered, a slight amusement disclosing itself in his voice. 'But come with me and you shall see for yourself.'

We took the elevated to Forty-Second Street and walked over to Broadway. On the southwest corner, one of the detectives in plain clothes, whom I recognized as Murphy, was lazily scanning the passersby.

'How many, Murphy?' Crewe asked him.

'Two hundred and seventy-three, sir,' Murphy responded. 'Seventy-four,' he added, as a man hurried by, almost brushing into us.

'You're keeping the three parts of the day separate, Murphy?' asked Crewe. 'Good. Keep up your count and report to me tomorrow morning at five. At the stroke of midnight you vacate your post.'

'Five o'clock till midnight seems long hours, Crewe,' I said.

'It is. But it's only for three days, and the men are trained for such periods of work. Besides, they understand that they share in the reward and, somehow or other, I've been able to persuade them that they can trust in me. I happened to know something of the past history of each,' he added, smiling.

'You remember them all?'

'Assuredly. I told Murphy that in 1909 he was on duty at the intersection of Eighty-First Street and Broadway when the explosion occurred in the subway, and that he helped to carry up the victims. I reminded him of an unpleasant little incident connected with a fruit peddler's license that year. Langton, it's a fine thing to remember faces. I've convinced all four men, I believe, that I have some *supernatural* knowledge about them — and merely because, in my strolls about the city, I've encountered almost all the police force at some time or another, and remember them. But let's hurry southward. Our next objective is the Brooklyn Bridge.'

We emerged at the bridge subway station, in front of which, leaning against the railings of the City Hall Park, I recognized O'Rourke. He straightened himself and came up to us.

'Eighty-seven this morning and thirty-nine up to this moment,' he said.

'I see you know your business,' Crewe responded. 'Don't let anyone pass, O'Rourke. Remember, your share of the reward will pay the mortgage on that house of yours.'

O'Rourke leaped back in astonishment. His mouth opened and he looked at Crewe in amazement.

'Don't jump like that,' said Crewe. 'You frighten me. I mean the house in Jamaica.' Then, as we turned away, he added: 'I saw him talking to his wife one afternoon two years ago when he was off duty. It was a long shot, though — the house might have been paid for. Now for our other two.'

We took the elevated to Sixth Avenue and Twenty-Third Street, where we found Kelly looking ostentatiously into a shop window.

'Very good,' said Crewe, slapping him upon the back. 'You saw us coming? Some men are too dense to know that one can see the passersby just as well when they're reflected in a plate-glass window. Happily, the precaution is unnecessary, but I'm glad to see so much intelligent zeal in your work, Kelly. You're keeping the numbers separate?'

'Seventy and thirty — thirty-one this instant, sir,' said Kelly, and we moved away. A cross-town street car and a brisk walk soon landed us at the Fourteenth Street subway entrance, where Cohen was seated in a shoeblack's chair getting a polish.

'Sixty-eight and twenty-seven, sir,' he whispered as we passed by. Crewe nodded almost imperceptibly, and we turned back into Union Park. At Crewe's invitation, we took our seats upon a bench.

'And now, Langton,' he said, 'you want to know what this apparently unintelligible process means, and I'll let you into the secret. You may have observed that I chose four points in New York at which to station my detectives. The selection of those points was influenced by two causes. In the first place, they're the four chief places where men walk, by preference, on one side of the street alone, and consequently it's easier to count the passersby than if my men had to watch both sides of the street. At the juncture of Broadway and Forty-Second Street, everybody who's not bent upon business — and Rowell is distinctly a pleasure-seeker these days — walks on the west side of the street, because extensive building operations are in progress upon the east side. At our southern point, the subway entrance to Brooklyn Bridge, almost everyone enters and emerges on the City Hall side. At Sixth Avenue and Twenty-Third Street, our populace walks on the south side, because that side of the thoroughfare is devoted to large stores whose windows hold a tempting array of goods. And on Fourteenth Street, everybody walks on the south side in order to pass the numerous moving picture shows, which afford a spectacle of some interest, even to the man who affects to despise them.

'So much for the minor reason for my selection. Now for the major reason. These four points embrace practically the entire amusement and shopping district of the city. Where would a stranger go, an Englishman without a friend in town, but in this region? Would he seek his amusement in the dreary wastes of Harlem? Would he moon all day in Central Park, a prey to his thoughts? No, Langton, it's the surest prophecy in the world that Rowell, a victim of a bad conscience and an over-full purse, spends all his waking life within this region. And it's safe to say that he alternates between the Fourteenth Street region and Broadway, with a preference for Broadway. Now I've told you enough for the present. Dine with me on Friday evening at seven. I'll be in the lobby of the Hotel Memphis, and I think I shall be able to afford you an evening's entertainment.'

I knew better than to attempt to question my companion further, but I was in a fever of anxiety during the three ensuing days to understand Crewe's purpose. His reasoning was excellent upon an abstract plane. But how did this counting of faces go toward the capture of Rowell?

It was not until after dinner that my curiosity was gratified. Crewe rinsed his fingers in the silver dinner bowl, folded his napkin leisurely, and took from his pocket a pad of paper upon which were jotted several series of figures.

'Do you believe in statistics, Langton?' he asked abruptly.

'I've heard it said that they can prove anything.'

'They can, but not in the derogatory

sense you mean. Are you aware that, while small numbers are apt to fluctuate, in the aggregate they're practically unvarying? For instance, in the gambling palace at Monte Carlo, red may turn up fifty times more than black during a single day. But in a week the relative numbers will be almost equal. In a month they'll be practically equal, while at the end of a year there is usually hardly a sensible difference between the number of times that each has to its credit.

'Take life insurance. Individually, a human life is a most uncertain thing. But when you take ten thousand lives, you can state with mathematical precision that a definite number of these ten thousand persons will die at thirty, a certain number at forty, increasing numbers at fifty, and so on, until at the age of ninety-six, the last survivor perishes.

'Langton, I've simply applied this fact to the search for Rowell. What do we know of him? That he's an average-appearing Englishman and wears a blue serge suit. Undoubtedly he possesses other suits, but equally surely he'll be astute enough to wear blue, as it will differentiate him less than a suit with check or stripe patterns. This time his own cleverness assists in his undoing.

'My orders to those detectives were to count all the men in blue serge suits who passed them, excluding those whose age obviously excluded the possibility of their being Rowell. I ordered each man to make three lists — one for the morning hours, one for the afternoon, and one for the evening, up to twelve o'clock, after which the number of men in blue serge suits abroad is too limited for us to draw deductions from it. Here are the results:

'Passing Forty-Second Street: morning, 156; afternoon, 112; evening, 177. Total, 445. Passing the Brooklyn Bridge subway entrance: morning, 84; afternoon, 46; evening, 88. Total, 218. Passing Twenty-Third Street and Sixth Avenue: morning, 72; afternoon, 28; evening 70. Total, 170. Passing the subway entrance on Four-teenth Street: morning, 80; afternoon, 29; evening, 85. Total, 194. What do you deduce from these figures, Langton?'

'That a surprisingly small number of

men in blue serge suits emerge from the entrance to Brooklyn Bridge during the rush hours,' I answered.

'My dear Langton, you're flying off on a tangent. That isn't relative to the matter at all. Many take surface cars from Brooklyn and never pass the subway entrance. And Brooklyn is barred from our consideration. No, do you not see that at three points, the morning and evening traffic is astonishingly even? At Twenty-Third Street, 72 men pass in the morning and 70 in the evening. At the Fourteenth Street subway, 80 pass in the morning and 85 in the evening. At the Brooklyn Bridge subway entrance, 84 pass in the morning and 88 in the evening. Therefore we can proceed by striking out like figures on either side of our equation. These men in blue serge suits are office workers; they go and return by the same routes morning and evening. Emphatically, Rowell won't be found among this lot.

'At our northern point, Forty-Second Street, the conditions aren't quite so even. The men who pass in the morning number 156; in the evening 177 — a difference of

21. Now we begin to see daylight at last after working out these figures. We have to postulate the average man, the average unemployed man. Let's discover him from among the figures that we have left.

'Passing Twenty-Third Street in the afternoon, 28. Passing Fourteenth Street in the afternoon, 29. Passing the Brooklyn Bridge subway entrance in the afternoon, 46. But these latter we must disregard, as they're in the office district and are probably all workers.

'Our final statement, therefore, is that 28 men stroll of an afternoon from Twenty-Third Street to Fourteenth Street, where their numbers are augmented to 29. During the same period of the day, 112 men stroll up Broadway to Forty-Second Street, where by nightfall their numbers have increased to 177. Therefore, our average man will most assuredly be found somewhere in the theater district after the lights are lit. Rowell will be there tonight; I've just demonstrated this infallibility. Come, Langton — we're going to arrest him.'

I rose in bewilderment. Crewe's figures were falling over one another in my brain, and only one clear impression remained to me: that Rowell was obligingly waiting to tumble into our arms at the juncture of Forty-Second Street and Broadway. But surely that was a case in which one could not predicate the individual from the universal. Suppose he *had* decided to vary his itinerary for that evening; suppose he had gone home. Suppose he were sick, or at a theater, or restaurant. Suppose he had taken a fancy to sit in Central Park until the hour of midnight. Suppose he had escaped from the city and were at that moment speeding westward.

I glanced at Crewe. His face was resolute, set into its usual decisive lines. I had known him to solve greater mysteries — but always by his optical gift, never by pure induction. And I could not help feeling that there was a sad disillusionment in store for him.

At Forty-Second Street and Broadway we found Murphy on duty. Crewe drew him aside. I saw him whisper and saw Murphy touch the pocket of his coat. I heard the clink of steel. Then we three posted ourselves immediately beneath a bright streetlight and engaged in trivial conversation, as if we were three pleasure-seekers.

Half an hour must have gone by. At least fifty men in blue suits had passed us, a good half of whom might have been the missing cashier. All at once I saw Crewe touch Murphy's arm, and the two swung round and walked leisurely after a good-looking young fellow who was passing briskly up the thoroughfare. At the Forty-Second Street crossing he hesitated a moment, pulled out his cigarette case, and began to smoke. A streetlight beat down full upon his face and shoulders.

Crewe went up to him, fixed his eyes upon his collar, signaled Murphy, and touched his captive on the shoulder. The man started violently and let his cigarette fall.

'We want *you*, Mr. Rowell,' said Crewe. At the same instant Murphy snapped the handcuffs upon the cashier's wrists.

'I can understand that your mathematical reasoning would, as you said, enable you to postulate the average man,' I remarked to Crewe subsequently. 'But how could you *positively* identify Rowell among your 117 men in blue serge? And how could you know for sure that he was strolling up Broadway?'

'I didn't. It wasn't until I got him under the streetlights that I was able to pronounce him Rowell with certitude.'

'But how?'

'Do you remember the cashier's seat at the London bank, with its projecting grille?'

'Yes.'

'Do you remember that the manager confirmed for us they had had an unusual quantity of sunshine in London?'

'I do.'

'Do you remember that Rowell wore a blue serge suit?'

'How could I not? You've had the detectives counting them for days!'

'Don't you know that blue serge fades?'

'In sunlight?'

'Precisely. And in consequence, since he sat always in the same spot, and bent over his counter at the same elevation, the bars of the grille would leave thin stripes of unfaded material in the discolored cloth. Langton, to your eyes Rowell's suit may have looked like any other man's suit, but to mine his breast and shoulders were striped like a zebra's.'

'How did you know he wouldn't order a new suit? He might have bought one ready-made.'

'The ready-made clothing trade is exclusively an American institution,' Crewe answered suavely. 'No Englishman can *ever* be persuaded that he'll look like anything but a tramp in a suit of ready-made clothes.'

7

The Whirl of Death

Although the authorities on both sides of the water hushed up the affair to the best of their ability, a few persons are cognizant of the facts relating to Benedict Shay, the celebrated inventor. He was brought to trial in England under the name he had assumed — which is immaterial here — and, being found insane by the jury, was sentenced to Broadmoor, which means that he will spend the remainder of his life in that excellent asylum which England maintains for her insane criminals. That the prisoner was Shay was known to less than a dozen persons, of whom Crewe and myself were two, the judge and the public prosecutor two more, and the administrators of Shay's estate in America the remainder.

When Shay disappeared from Baltimore after betraying signs of a complete mental breakdown, my services were requisitioned by his friends, who were desirous of having him brought back and placed under the care of the best physicians. It was known that Shay had sailed for England, but there all trace of him had been lost. Shay's career had been a romantic one.

Beginning as a newsboy, he had made discovery after discovery in engineering and the kindred sciences, whose patents had brought him fame and wealth. It was after his improvement of the turbine, a task at which he labored incessantly for months, that the mental collapse occurred. He went crazy over perpetual motion, produced the most bizarre — and, of course, entirely worthless — machines, declared that his failure to have these taken up was due to a plot, developed homicidal tendencies and, the day before his intended apprehension, sailed for London upon a British ship, thus removing himself from American jurisdiction. Although his whereabouts were unknown, it was obvious that he would be found in close touch with engineering men across the Atlantic, and I had little doubt that I should readily locate him, after which the real task of inducing him to sail for America would begin.

In spite of the facility of my task, I thought it wise to consult Peter Crewe as soon as I reached England. He had been in London for several weeks when I arrived, and my first task was to call on him and ask his assistance in locating the object of my search.

'Shay?' queried Crewe thoughtfully. 'I must've seen his photograph. Oldish man, clean-shaven, clear eyes, iron-gray hair?'

'No,' I replied, laughing. 'You're thinking of Edison. Shay is a short, stout man, about forty-five, with a straight nose, eyes wrinkled at the corners, a trick of screwing up his forehead when he speaks to you — '

'I've seen him twice during the last week,' Crewe answered. 'I noticed him particularly, because I recognized him as a man whom I once saw entering the engineering exhibition at Madison Square Garden in New York, and wearing his hat awry. I've seen him twice, and curiously enough, each time in the same place and at the same time. It was in the Earl's

Court Road at eight in the morning, and he was walking briskly in the direction of Kensington. I've been in the habit of passing through that region at an early hour on my way to my brother's office, and the coincidence of this double meeting impressed me greatly.'

'Then how can we find him?'

'Why, let's be in the same spot tomorrow at the same hour, and I should say that we should run an excellent chance,' Crewe answered with his brusque common sense.

We followed Crewe's suggestion, but though we perambulated the Earl's Court Road for several mornings in succession, we did not encounter Shay.

'Have you been to the engineering papers and the big firms?' Crewe asked.

'No. I want to avoid doing so if possible,' I said. 'I don't want the facts of my mission to become known.'

'Unless we meet the man face to face, I hardly think we're likely to find him,' Crewe replied. 'There are several million people in the metropolitan district of London, Langton.'

It did indeed seem to be a case in which Crewe's optical powers would prove unavailing. We walked slowly back past the entrance to Earl's Court Exhibition, discussing the matter. All at once a placard caught my eye. It stated that on the following night a great industrial exhibition would be opened, in which engines and engine tools would have a prominent display. I caught Crewe by the arm. 'We have him!' I exclaimed exultantly. 'He'll be here for certain.'

Crewe agreed with me and, highly elated, we retraced our steps homeward. On the next evening we joined the crowds at the exhibition entrance and were shortly admitted. We passed through the spacious grounds — where scenic railways, loop-the-loop and shoot-the-chutes arrangements vied with the booths of fortune-tellers and those sideshows dear to the exhibition crowds — and entered the machinery hall. The first person who caught my eye was Shay. He was standing, gazing intently at the numerous mechanical inventions, but he seemed to sense my presence and, turning around, came toward me with an outstretched hand.

'Glad to see you in London, Langton,' he said cordially. I introduced him to Crewe, and we passed the usual platitudes concerning the weather and England's value as a holiday resort. His conversation certainly seemed rational enough. It was not until we spoke of machinery that Shay's aberration became manifest.

'What brings you to London, Langton?' he asked. 'Holiday-making?'

'A little matter of business,' I answered evasively. 'And you?'

Shay's manner changed. His face became contorted, and his excitement was intense. 'To gain the recognition that I'm denied by jealous competitors in America,' he cried. 'Langton, I've made the greatest discovery of the century — perpetual motion. I've invented a machine that will harness the sun's heat and provide the earth with a substitute for coal. It will supply unlimited power and abolish half the electrical mechanisms of the day. And why won't anyone listen to me, either here or in my own country? Because the interests are allied in a dastardly plot to crush me!' he shouted. 'They prefer their present wealth to benefiting the human race. Half the water companies would go bankrupt, Langton, for I can draw rain from the clouds, I can bring fire out of the earth — I can work miracles with *my machine*.'

'How is it made?' asked Crewe.

Shay's face became instantly composed. He looked at him in a cunning manner. 'I'm not as easy as *that*,' he said with a jeer. 'But I'll tell you the principle of the secret. It's a combination of centrifugal and centripetal power. I'm perfecting a few investigations,' he went on, smiling inscrutably, 'which will bring the mechanism to its highest point of utility. And then, if the world scorns me, I'll give some practical demonstrations that will *never* be forgotten.'

'Shay,' I interposed, 'I have a message for you from your brother; he asked me to deliver it if I should come across you. He wants you to try and get back next month to take a contract for equipping his factory. He says that your presence would be necessary — '

Shay squared his shoulders, threw back his head and burst into a roar of malignant laughter. 'So they sent you after me, Langton,' he guffawed. 'You must think me easy. You want to get me back,' he continued, catching me by the coat lapels, 'to put me in a lunatic asylum. That's the last move of the interests, along with my brother — my poor brother, whom they've corrupted with their filthy gold. Langton, you can't extradite a man for lunacy. If I were as raving as you believe, you couldn't touch me when the British flag protects me. *Get out!*' he concluded with singular violence. 'I'll have no more to say to you.'

'My dear Mr. Shay — ' I protested, feeling uncommonly foolish.

'*Get out!*' he roared. 'You *and* your friend. If I set eyes on either of you again, I'll fix you. I'll mash you small; I'll break every bone in your bodies and I'll deposit them in the middle of the Earl's Court Road with the consistency of a plum pudding.'

'Well, Langton, the next move is up to you,' said Crewe, laughing, as we strolled away. 'He's an uncommonly intelligent madman, and the prospect is that he'll land in some British asylum instead of running into the net you so patently exposed for him.'

The chances of fulfilling my mission did look small to me. I went to bed very dejected, and awoke still more so. Opening my morning paper, I saw a three-column headline in black letters. In England that means more than in America. The story gave the details of a murder. The body of an elderly man had been found, every bone broken to pieces. Even a fall from a rooftop could not have effected that terrific destruction, said the account, for the head was driven right into the ground. The only possible explanation was that the victim had fallen several thousand feet from a hot air balloon or other aerial contrivance.

But what horrified me was this: The body had been found five hundred yards from Earl's Court Exhibition, and in the middle of the Earl's Court Road. The thought of Shay rushed into my mind. I hurried round to Crewe.

'I think the balloon explanation the only possible one,' he said, when I had unfolded my fears. 'You're overwrought, Langton. Put Shay out of your mind; his words were the ravings of a madman.'

But the next day another similar death was chronicled. The body of a man had been found wedged into the wall of an empty house in Bromley Street, about the same distance from Earl's Court grounds, but in an opposite direction. It had been flung with such terrific violence that it had passed through six inches of bricks and mortar and lodged in the front of the house. The human form was barely recognizable.

This time Crewe smiled no longer. 'One can but fall *vertically* from a balloon,' he mused. 'But this man must have been shot from a twelve-inch gun. Langton, I think I'll look for your friend Shay again. But this time we'll avoid his recognition.'

That night, accordingly, we went into the Earl's Court grounds. We loitered in the vicinity of the machinery exhibition, but there was no trace of Shay. After a while we strolled through the gardens, listened to the bands, and inspected a number of sideshows from the outside. Suddenly I felt Crewe pinch my arm.

We were passing the aerial ride. Everybody, probably, has ridden in this contrivance at some time or other. One gets into a boat, suspended, with a number of other boats, from a central pole by long stays of steel. A mechanism underground sets the boats revolving through the air. As they swing further and further out they tilt inward, until one rides at a dizzy pace almost upon his side. If the machine were not operating one would fall to the ground below, but the force of centrifugal motion keeps one in the boat as water stays in a bucket whirled round the head. We were passing this contrivance, I say, when, looking up in response to Crewe's pinch, I saw that the operator was Shay.

I knew him, though he wore a mechanic's cloth cap and a workman's clothes. More than that, he knew me. I saw an expression of unconquerable hate pass over his features and, fairly frightened, hurried away with Crewe. At a newspaper kiosk we saw the familiar black headlines in an evening paper. I purchased one. It was the usual story: a third body had been found, three hundred yards from the exhibition grounds, upon a rooftop. It had knocked down three chimneys and torn off a cornice, and had doubtless been thrown there during the preceding night.

Crewe was very thoughtful when we sat together in my rooms that night. 'It *can't* be due to Shay,' he cried. 'That story of his about an irresistible power is absurd. And yet, Langton — what does it mean? I can't fathom it.'

His glance fell upon my bookshelf and he rose to his feet. 'I see you have an enlarged map of London — an ordnance survey, I believe,' he said. 'I saw it yesterday as we were passing out of the door. Yes, here it is. Let's investigate.'

He spread the great sheets on the table, turning them until he reached that of the Earl's Court region. Every house and street was accurately depicted upon this monumental record of patient industry. 'The first body was found *here*,' he said, piercing the paper with a pin. 'And the second in the Bromley Road — *here*. The third on the roof of 55 Quantock Street — *here*. Now we have three-fourths of a circle if we join these pinholes by a faint line. Upon the fourth side — '

He ceased, for through the open window we heard a newsboy shouting in the street. 'Another body found,' he cried. ''Orrible discovery in Preston Road. All the details.'

We raced downstairs and bought a copy. Another corpse had been located in a branch of a tree in Preston Road. Crewe hurried back to the map and pricked the spot. '*I have it!*' he shouted. 'Four points on a circumference. Find the center. Langton, I'm going to spoil your map.' He connected the points and, using his thumb and finger as a pair of compasses, completed the circle with his fingernail, tracing the nail marks on the paper with a pencil afterward. Then he pointed to the center, and I sprang to my feet, choking.

The center of the circle was the bandstand in the Earl's Court grounds. And the bandstand was not twenty yards from the aerial ride. 'What does it mean?' I cried.

'Take your hat, take your hat, Langton,' said Crewe impatiently. 'We'll find out before morning. You know the entrance to the Exhibition which leads past the chutes to the bandstand?'

'No. I didn't think there was one.'

'I mean the low wall that one can vault over,' said Crewe impatiently. 'The gap left by the workmen who are repairing the wall. Oh, Langton, why the devil can't you use your eyes? We passed it yesterday on that omnibus. Never mind. Listen! The Exhibition closes at seven. We vault that wall at 11:30, when all the people have left. We hide in that cluster of trees — you didn't see them, those Japanese laurel shrubs? — well, take my word for it, they *are* there, and we hide in them till midnight, when everybody has gone home. Why not wait till midnight before vaulting the wall — ? My good Langton, at midnight the people leave the restaurant opposite, since the law forbids them to purchase drinks after that hour. No, I can understand you didn't notice the restaurant.'

I glanced at the clock as I put on my hat. It was half past ten. There was just time to reach our objective comfortably, but none to spare. We descended the stairs, went into the street and took a motor omnibus for Earl's Court, where we got down.

To cross the wall was simple, and we were soon ensconced in the clump of laurel shrubs. Earl's Court was empty of its throngs, and the proprietors of the booths and amusement shows were wending their tired ways homeward. After ten minutes more we remained practically the sole inmates of the gardens.

'Langton,' said Crewe, 'we've *got* to find what's going to occur at that aerial ride tonight. I want you to wait here for me while I go forward and investigate whether or not our masquerading engineer has closed up his property and left. If I need you, I shall blow my police whistle. Wait half an hour, then come cautiously in search of me.'

I had no watch, and the minutes passed like hours. Once or twice, shivering there alone in the darkness, I fancied I heard faint calls from the direction of the bandstand. But the whistle did not blow. At last, wearied of my delay, and with cramped limbs that demanded stretching, I set off toward our objective. I passed the chutes and the bandstand. The place was wholly deserted; not even a watchman was to be seen anywhere. As I drew toward the aerial ride, I noticed a faint glow from the basement in which the mechanism was located. Over my head the boats hung idly and emptily against the sky. Then —

An arm was round my throat, compressing it so that I could utter no sound. My head was forced back till the vertebrae felt on the point of breaking; and I was staring into the malignant eyes of Shay. He was quite mad — furiously and incoherently mad — and as he held me in his powerful grip, he babbled out his triumph.

'I've got your friend,' he cried. 'But *you'll* come first, and he'll wait in the engine house. I'll mash you, you sneaking lawyer. I'll smash you; I'll crush you into a plum pudding and lay you down in

Earl's Court Road. I've proved it,' he went on, gesticulating wildly with one hand but never releasing his stranglehold. 'One more, two more bodies found tomorrow, and all London will go crazy over my instrument. You don't want to die, Langton? Why, you will be a martyr to science, you will prove the truth of what I told the world, you will assist me to overcome the interests who have fought down my invention for the benefit of the human race. Come along, come along, come *joyfully*, Langton. I'm going to explain it to you before you go through the air.'

I was as helpless as an infant in his clasp. Still throttling me, he dragged me up the flight of wooden steps that led to the aerial ride and deposited me in one of the motionless boats that swung round a wooden platform. Then, gibbering like a madman and uttering meaningless cries, he gagged me and began binding my arms and legs with a coil of cord.

'You know the principle of this flight,' he said in calmer tones. 'You know how the centrifugal force keeps the boats out

153

from the center of the pole and keeps you in that boat. Oh, what a ride you'll have! We never send our patrons at a speed greater than twenty miles an hour, but my perfected engine will work up to one hundred and twenty. Langton, you'll go whizzing round and round at the speed of an express train, and you'll be horizontal with the ground and the boat will go sailing upon her side — and yet you won't fall out because of the centrifugal power.'

He gave one last twist to the cords that bound me and glared into my eyes. 'But suppose I suddenly shut off the engine? What then?' he asked. A smile flickered across his face. 'I'll tell you, Langton,' he said. 'What happens when you whirl the pail of water round and round your head and suddenly stop? What happens to the water? Does it stay in the pail? Or does it go through the air? Langton, *you're going through the air*. The sudden cessation of the centrifugal force, converted into energy, will throw you just about as hard as a cannonball.

'You might land in the Earl's Court Road, or you might land in Preston Road, or in Bromley Street. I can't promise for certain, but my aim *is* improving, and I can assure you of four hundred yards' clean traveling over the rooftops.' He ceased and broke into reviling. He struck me several times, kicked me with his heels, and in his uncontrollable rage seemed on the point of murdering me. Then, tearing himself away with a shout of final defiance, he left me.

I heard the mechanism begin whirring in the engine house and felt the boat begin to move. It glided gently at first, but soon its motion was accelerated. Now I was flying high in the air over the grounds; faster and faster I flew, till the trees, the buildings and the night shadows were nothing but a blur under me. The speed was inconceivable! It was as though I were lashed to the engine of some train which spun on its circular course at about twice the speed of the Chicago Flyer. My brain reeled, my senses were deserting me; terror, even, fled from my benumbed consciousness, and I waited calmly for that supreme moment when the power suddenly arrested. I should be sent flying out of the boat and through the air, over the revolving housetops.

Each moment seemed an eternity. Would that culmination never arrive? And even as I wondered, I felt a shock that jarred each nerve in me; a blinding light, an awful sound in my ears — and I lost consciousness.

When I opened my eyes, I was still in the boat. But my bonds were unfastened and Crewe was bending over me, rubbing my chafed and tingling limbs. My head swum dizzily.

'It's all right, Langton,' he said cheerily. 'The watchmen have him under guard in the engine house.'

I stared at Crewe, hardly yet conscious of my surroundings, memory slowly filtering back through her accustomed courses.

'What happened to you?' I muttered, striving to recall the occurrences of that period after Crewe's departure.

He sat by me in the boat and rubbed my arms and legs briskly. 'Why, Langton, I must confess that the maniac outwitted me. He came upon me from behind as silently as a cat, and choked me into insensibility. When I opened my eyes I found myself bound in the engine house. I knew exactly what sort of devilry he was up to, and I surmised that you'd be trapped as easily as I. Presently he came back; he was so intent on your destruction that he didn't seem to notice me, but from his incoherent mumbling I learned that he had you fastened in one of the boats. He threw on the lever which starts the mechanism and, as the machinery began to work and the speed accelerated, he stood there, rubbing his hands and chuckling, with me bound hand and foot not ten paces away, immediately behind a dynamo.

'From where I lay I saw the speed indicator creep up from nothing toward the century mark. I understood that when it reached one hundred and twenty, the maximum, the fiend would throw the lever back and send you flying into perdition. I strove to free myself. I got one arm loose, but that was all. Then I saw an iron bolt lying not five feet from me, and somehow — I can't imagine how — I managed to reach it. Just then the end came. I saw the indicator needle reach the end of the dial. Shay flung back the lever with a shriek of joy, and then, maddened by the thought that your life had been sacrificed, I managed to catch his ankle as he leaped back, and brought him to the ground; then I stunned him with the bolt. I found a penknife in his pocket, cut my bonds, and summoned the night watchmen by my cries. But I dared not hope to find you still in the boat.'

'But *why* am I still in the boat?' I cried. 'Why did I not go flying through the air when he stopped the machinery?'

'Why,' said Crewe, smiling faintly, 'you owe your life to a most providential oversight on the part of our maniac. In his half-witted fury, instead of merely strapping your arms to your sides, he accidentally passed the cords several times around the iron stay that holds the boat in position.'

8

The Crooked Seam

The story told me by Sir Arnold Blythe appeared to contain the elements of some mystery, the solution of which required the aid of Peter Crewe. I therefore made an appointment at my office for the following day, when the two men were to meet.

'Now, sir, will you repeat your story as you told it to me yesterday?' I said to the Englishman, after the formalities of the introduction had been complied with.

Sir Arnold was an Englishman of international reputation as an expert on ancient textiles. He had, in fact, come to New York at the invitation of Phineas Boone, the multi-millionaire, to assist him in the classification of his rare collection of Oriental rugs.

'You had a valuable rug destroyed recently by vandals?' asked Crewe before the Englishman could commence his story. 'There was an account of it in last Sunday's papers, together with illustrations of the mutilated corner.'

'Yes, but that isn't what I wish to speak about,' replied Sir Arnold. 'The matter is in the hands of the police, who hold out every hope of discovering the criminal. I want to tell you about my dog.'

Crewe leaned back in his chair and allowed Sir Arnold to proceed with his story.

'The fact is,' he said, 'that both my wife and I are being shadowed by Syrians. She's almost prostrated with fear and anxiety, and the matter must be cleared up at all hazards. And their chief objective seems to be my dog — or my wife's dog, rather.'

'Recently acquired?' asked Crewe.

'Only last week,' Sir Arnold replied. 'Lady Blythe was passing down Broadway on Thursday afternoon and had just reached its intersection with Thirty-Sixth Street, when her attention was attracted by a Syrian man who was offering some puppies for sale on the corner. My wife is fond of animals and of an impulsive nature. One of the creatures came fawning toward her, and she couldn't resist the temptation to purchase it. The animal is only a mongrel, and the fellow demanded an undue price for it; finally he threw in a pretty Syrian dog blanket of modern make, but an excellent imitation of an old Persian weave. This clinched the bargain, and Lady Blythe bought the beast and took it home.

'On the following morning, when she had the creature on a leash in the park, she noticed that she was being followed by the same Syrian. She sat down upon a bench to rest and the man passed her, traversed a short distance, turned back and whistled. Immediately the dog broke from her control and set off at full speed toward its former owner. Happily a gentleman who had witnessed the occurrence gave chase, caught the beast and restored it to Lady Blythe, while the fellow succeeded in making his escape. Much upset by this occurrence, Lady Blythe returned home.

'The next day she took the dog out

again, but on reaching Fifty-Ninth Street once more perceived the same man following her. She was so unnerved at the sight that she called a taxi cab and came home and went to bed. That night a death threat was received. The dog must be delivered, blanket and all, at a certain spot the following day, or our lives would be forfeited.

'I called in the police, and it was arranged that a messenger should take the dog to the place agreed upon — but nobody arrived. However, on the next morning another letter was received by me. It was signed with a bloody hand and in effect repeated the former menace, but still more strongly. The creature is valueless, the blanket is worth at most two dollars, and I am wholly at a loss to understand the cause of this persecution.'

'This rug that was mutilated was cut with a pair of scissors,' said Crewe. 'Did not that strike you as strange?'

'I would prefer to discuss one thing at a time,' replied Sir Arnold. 'The mutilation of Mr. Boone's rug has nothing to do with the matter I've been speaking of.'

'Nevertheless, I'd like to hear about the rug,' persisted Crewe. 'There may be some immediate connection. Will you tell me, Sir Arnold, the circumstances of that affair?'

'There's *nothing* to tell, beyond what the papers *said*,' answered the Englishman testily. 'One of the rugs, a Persian textile of great antiquity, had a corner cut away with a pair of scissors, leaving a jagged tear. The act was perpetrated sometime after midnight on Wednesday, and the perpetrator succeeded in making his escape undetected.'

'The police have discovered no clue?'

'So far, none. They've searched every rug depository in the city in vain. It seems evident that the criminal has succeeded in making good his escape.'

'But you said the police hold out every hope of discovering him.'

'Yes. Of course, sooner or later the mutilated fragment will reappear somewhere, probably in the possession of a peddler. But to come back to the dog — '

'I have here a photograph of the rug,' persisted Crewe, drawing a sheet of newspaper from his breast pocket. 'The matter interested me exceedingly.' He handed it to Sir Arnold. 'What are those arabesques immediately above the tear?' he asked.

'Meaningless and conventional Persian borders,' answered the Englishman. 'They're a feature of all rugs of a certain century. That border was cut off by the marauder, apparently aimlessly. But now, sir, I insist upon discussing this affair of the dog. What do you advise me to do?'

'Let me see him and his blanket,' Crewe answered. 'When would it be convenient for us to call?'

'You can come back with me at once,' Sir Arnold answered. 'And if you can solve the mystery, I shall be most grateful, and Mr. Boone will — '

Crewe waved away the suggestion of the reward. He rose and took his hat. 'Are you ready, Langton?' he asked.

I rose, and we followed Sir Arnold out of my office. We descended to the street and took a limousine to the millionaire's town house, which was temporarily occupied by the Englishman and his wife.

Once inside, Crewe asked to be taken to the collection of textiles.

Sir Arnold led us into the chamber in which they were spread out for classification. The mutilated rug was not at first apparent, for the injury had been much slighter than we had supposed. Only one extreme corner had been removed, having been cut out in a zig-zag fashion with a pair of blunt scissors, and the woolen threads were curled and warped over the texture. Crewe studied the rug long and earnestly.

'The arabesque was in the part removed?' he asked. 'Then why was there no similar border woven into the fabric upon the other corners?'

Here Sir Arnold felt himself upon safe ground. This was his province. He turned upon Crewe somewhat pompously. 'My good man,' he said, 'the craze for evenness of design did not, most fortunately, afflict the Persians of the date when this fabric was made. The weaver chose to place a border upon one corner of the rug alone, and that fact in itself fixes the date of it beyond all doubt. And now, if you've quite satisfied your curiosity, will you look at my dog, or not?'

Before Crewe could answer, there came a scampering of feet along the passage, and the animal bounded into the room with many demonstrations of affection for its new master. It was a curly mongrel of no particular breed. Trailing from its back was the dog blanket. Crewe stooped, unfastened it, and placed it upon the table.

'And this, you say, is of *modern* workmanship?' he asked. 'What do those Persian words signify?'

'That,' replied Sir Arnold, 'literally translated, is: 'May the wealth of Arziban and the treasures of Mulik's Castle go to the possessor.' It's a purely conventional expression, woven into their blankets by the modern Syrians in imitation of the ancients, and wishes prosperity to the owner.'

'And the blanket can't possibly be of the same date as the rug?' asked Crewe.

Sir Arnold smiled in a patronizing way. 'You can take it from me,' he said, 'that there's no possible connection between the rug and the blanket. They were made several hundred years apart. Do you mean to suggest that the man who mutilated the rug sold me the blanket?'

'Offhand, I should say that it's extremely unlikely,' answered Crewe.

'Then will you tell me, sir, the meaning of this persecution, and why the former owner of the dog desires him back again, and why the blanket is an essential feature of the demand?'

Suddenly Sir Arnold's brows contracted. He staggered slightly and, raising his hand, pointed through the open window into Lexington Avenue. '*My God!* There he is, *again!*' he cried.

We looked in the direction indicated and saw a man of swarthy countenance standing on the opposite side of the road, watching us intently. As soon as he saw that he was perceived, he shook his hand menacingly toward us and leaped into a passing cab. There was no possibility of capturing him; before we could have reached the door he would have been out of sight.

'My explanation,' I said, when our host

had recovered from the unexpected shock, 'would be that you're the victims of an insane Syrian who imagines that you're keeping his property from him, and, having mutilated your rug, he now desires the dog's blanket.'

'But he *sold* my wife the dog,' cried Sir Arnold. 'And he wants the dog as well. Confound it all, there's no sense in the affair.'

'Let me advise you,' said Crewe. 'Send the dog out by a messenger boy, with instructions that it is to be delivered to the first man who asks for it.'

Sir Arnold was thoroughly exasperated. 'That's similar to the advice of the police,' he cried. 'The dog is *my* property, and let me tell you, I would rather be murdered than give over one jot of my rights. Do you think I'm going to be cheated by a dog peddler? If that's all you can advise me, I might as well never have consulted you.'

'Then let me warn you that your life is in grave danger,' answered Crewe. 'Think the matter over and, for your wife's sake, if not for your own, alter your mind.

Good afternoon.' He clapped on his hat and strode toward the door, leaving me the task of mollifying the Englishman, which I did with only partial success.

'It would have been impossible to assist that pig-headed old gentleman,' said Crewe to me as we strolled homeward. 'The only thing to do is to await developments.'

'Do you think that the matter of the rug and the blanket are connected?' I asked him.

'Unquestionably, and what the Syrian wants is not the dog but the blanket.'

'But he sold it to him,' I cried, almost as exasperated as Sir Arnold had been himself when uttering the same protest.

'That makes it most improbable that the man who sold the dog was the same man that mutilated the rug. To be frank with you, Langton, my sympathies are more than half with the latter. But as for the scoundrel dog-seller, who betrayed his friend's confidence — if we can find him and have him lodged in jail, we shall not only put an end to the persecution but be enabled to restore the mutilated fragment to Sir Arnold.'

'Do you suspect where it is?' I asked.

'I know where it is.'

'Then why don't you restore it to its owner?'

Crewe stopped short and regarded me benignly. 'Because,' he said, 'if I did so, his life wouldn't be worth three days' purchase. It's one of those cases where I must sacrifice my reputation as a detective to save my client. I hope that his dog *is* stolen, and that the *blanket* is stolen and is *never* found. Unless we can find the dog-seller,' he added. 'That would be the most satisfactory conclusion of all. Come, let's look for him.'

'Where? In the Syrian quarter?'

'As far as possible from the Syrian quarter,' answered Crewe. 'You remember him?'

I shook my head. 'I only caught a glimpse of him through the window,' I protested.

'But you saw that he was dressed in blue, that he was freshly shaved, and that a pair of scissors bulged in his coat pocket?' asked Crewe with genuine eagerness.

'*You* may have seen those things. I saw only a ragged, dirty-looking man. But even if you can thus picture him, how will you locate him?'

'Well,' said Crewe, 'since the Syrian quarter lies far downtown, and he naturally wishes to avoid it — '

'Why should he wish to avoid it?'

'He won't leave that Lexington Avenue streetcar until it's well uptown. Now, since it's almost a matter of existence to him to keep watch upon Sir Arnold, he'll take the Lexington Avenue streetcar downtown again this evening. In consequence, all that we need do is to watch the cabs. And the best way will be to take a street car uptown and keep our eyes fixed on all the cabs that pass us.'

I could make neither head nor tail of Crewe's reasoning. But I knew that he had his own ways of procedure, and that however unintelligible they seemed to me, there was always some motive in them deeper than I could fathom. Accordingly, I went with him; we boarded the next street car that came along, and rode uptown. But though we passed many cars, there was no Syrian on them.

'He may, of course, have left the streetcar at some intermediate point,' he said. 'Well, sooner or later we'll have him. He'll probably attempt some disguise. The police will never know a Syrian from an Italian when he puts on a — '

He broke off, for whilst we were arrested at the stoplight, a newsboy sprung before us from a street corner and shoved an evening paper in our faces. Confronting me in big, staring headlines were the words 'Armenians in Duel. One Dead, One Dying.'

I snatched the paper from the boy, flung him some coins, and opened it. A few lines told the story. At One Hundred and Second Street, an unknown Armenian had been about to descend from a streetcar when another of his nationality leaped forward and plunged a knife into his throat. In his dying struggles the man had wrested the knife from the murderer and driven it home into his side, inflicting a fatal wound. The murdered man lived but a few moments; the murderer had been conveyed to the Unsectarian Hospital, where he lay dying.

He had refused to make an ante-mortem statement and had quickly lapsed into a coma, from which there was small probability of his awakening.

Crewe laid the paper down. 'That is the end of Sir Arnold's troubles,' he said. 'Come, let's go back to him.'

'You think the murdered men were the agents in all these happenings?' I asked.

'The murderer was the man who mutilated the rug,' he answered. 'The murdered man was the dog-seller who turned dog-stealer.'

We descended from the car in front of the Boone mansion and were speedily shown into the presence of Sir Arnold Blythe. He had been called from his dinner to receive us and was not disposed to be cordial. He took the paper from me with a gesture of weariness.

'Your rug mutilator has killed your dog-seller and lies dying,' said Peter Crewe. 'You'll no longer be troubled by either of them.'

Sir Arnold looked at him sardonically. 'That sounds good,' he said contemptuously. 'And now, since you've solved my problem with so much ingenuity, perhaps you'll be so kind as to restore the missing fragment of the rug to me.'

'I will, with pleasure,' answered Crewe, 'on one condition. Will you give me the dog blanket, to do with as I please?'

Sir Arnold indicated the blanket, which still lay upon the table. 'It's at your disposal,' he answered. 'And when, pray, may I expect the corner of the rug?'

'Immediately,' Crewe answered, drawing a little penknife from his pocket. He placed the point to the dog blanket and, with a few deft motions, cut it in half, diagonally. He held up one corner to Sir Arnold.

'Here's your missing fragment,' he said calmly.

I gasped. Sir Arnold gasped and stood, holding up the corner and stupidly gazing at it. Then, as in a dream, he walked over to the rug and placed the fragment against the fabric. It fitted exactly. It was, beyond all doubt, the missing corner. Presently he regained his self-possession.

'Well, Mr. Crewe,' he said, extending his hand, 'you've got the better of me.

And now the best amends that I can make to you is to ask you and your friend to join me at dinner. You will, I am sure, excuse the absence of Lady Blythe, who's still confined to her room. And if a bottle of '48 port can induce you to let me in on the secret, why . . . '

And the blunt, short-spoken Englishman proved the most delightful guest that I ever met. After the coffee had been brought in and the cigars lighted, Crewe expounded his theory to us.

'I don't pretend to be infallible,' he said, 'and it's possible that I'm wrong. If you can hit upon a happier solution, you're at liberty to adopt it, for it seems evident that the secret will perish with the murderer. But here's how the matter struck me.' He turned to me. 'Langton,' he said, 'what was your impression when you looked at the dog blanket?'

'That it was a dog blanket,' I replied. 'I saw nothing peculiar about it.'

'Did you not see that it had a crooked seam?'

I shook my head.

'Nor that the seam ran in a series of

zig-zags exactly corresponding to the zig-zag cut upon the mutilated rug?'

'I confess I didn't notice that.'

Crewe smiled tolerantly. 'Well,' he said, 'it's inexplicable to me that you should not have seen it. It seemed as plain as Pike's Peak that here was the missing fragment, right under the eyes of our host himself. And by the way, Sir Arnold, that dog blanket was not an imitation Persian, but as you see now, a genuine Persian. Moreover, the other half of the dog blanket had originally formed part of the original rug. In fact, in joining the two together, the Armenian, as we must now call the supposed Syrian, was merely replacing what had been removed centuries ago. Again, the arabesques — the supposed meaningless border — when joined to the other half proved to be the top portions of the Persian lettering. And this inscription, far from being a conventional wish, was in fact an ancient deed.

'To be succinct, the original rug was what's called a chirograph. It was a deed to 'the wealth of Arziban and the treasure of Mulik's Castle.' Each party to the deed kept one half of this woven document, which was slit in such a way that it could only be restored by the two owners fitting the halves together. This effectually prevented any forger from presenting a spurious fragment and claiming the property.

'Apparently, at some remote period the owner of one portion, fearing the loss of his piece of the rug, had it cunningly woven into one corner of the larger rug that came into your possession. But the legend lingered, and the family who inherited the other half of the deed always hoped to fit the two pieces together and thus someday recover the property. Finally, the one half came into the possession of the man whom we'll call Armenian A.

'In company with a friend, he set sail for New York to recover the second fragment of the deed. He learned that it was in Mr. Boone's possession and succeeded in stealing it. But he knew that the police would certainly discover it. There was no place to hide his trophy. Thereupon he hit upon a most ingenious scheme. Having sewn together the two fragments, thus completing the deed, he induced Armenian B, his friend, to place it over a dog and sell the creature upon the streets. He was to keep watch over the animal and, as soon as the police search had been concluded, to steal it *back* from its owner. By some extraordinary chance Lady Blythe became the purchaser of the dog and, with it, obtained the deed, in the form of a dog blanket.

'Meanwhile, Armenian B, the dog-seller, elated by the possibility of becoming sole owner of 'the wealth of Arziban and the treasures of Mulik's Castle,' gave his friend the slip. He wanted it all for himself. He didn't tell him who the purchaser was, or where she lived. Had he done so, the two together would indubitably have managed to regain the animal. Armenian B played a lone hand for several days, but the man whom he had betrayed succeeded in locating him this afternoon. The consequence of their encounter is now known to you. I think you'll no longer be troubled, Sir Arnold Blythe, and you can restore the rug to Mr. Phineas Boone intact, and with it the fabled properties in Persia, if he should care to put in a claim to them; for the other half of the deed is also *yours*.'

Suddenly Sir Arnold leaped out of his seat and came swiftly toward Peter Crewe. 'I've been wondering how you gained your knowledge of rugs,' he said. 'No man but one is able to controvert *my* judgment. Are you the Crewe who wrote a monograph on 'The Rugs of Kurdistan and the Lower Caucasus'?'

Here the conversation became too technical for me. I have no interest in the ravings of rug lovers. The rest of the evening passed, so far as I was concerned, less pleasantly.

9

The Scar

The solution of what I call the 'Pension Fraud Problem' was one of the hardest matters that ever fell to me in my capacity as a government investigator. Some of my work in London and New York had been brought to the attention of the departmental heads at Washington, D.C. — in particular the detection of the maniac Shay, a case in which I was singularly fortunate. I received a flattering offer of an inspectorship in the Pension Department, which was about this time much worried by the innumerable cases of fraud that were being continually discovered. And so, relinquishing my law practice in New York, I made Washington, D.C. my headquarters, from which I was sent out on various missions throughout the country, accomplishing them with what I may call, without self-flattery, tolerable success.

But the 'Pension Fraud Problem,' as I have named this particular case, baffled me; and at last, finding a solution impossible, I called in the aid of Peter Crewe. He responded to my appeal at once, and came to Washington, D.C., where I related to him the details of this affair.

The government is not overzealous in scrutinizing its rolls of army pensioners, and yet it did seem singular that a man who had been invalided out of the army in 1864 for physical disability, being then fifty-eight years of age, and having managed to enlist only because of the Union's desperate need of men, should still be hale and hearty and mulcting the government of $840 annually at the age of a hundred and four. Yet it was our task to prove the claim fraudulent — and I could not do so.

William Sears resided with his granddaughter, Mrs. Bolton, a middle-aged widow, on a little farm in Maryland. He was a hale old man and, though he claimed to have passed the century mark four years previously, he had the aspect of a man of some eighty-two or -three. They had moved to Maryland from Kansas a few years previously, and the government contention was that Mrs. Bolton, knowing that the death of her grandfather would entail the loss of the pension money, had contrived that this event should take place just after they moved from Kansas and before she arrived in Maryland, and had thereupon substituted another old man, but some years younger, in Sears' place.

But this was just what could not be proved. The old pensioner had taken up land in a pioneer district of Kansas, where he dwelt some fifteen miles from his nearest neighbor. Furthermore, he was crippled with rheumatism, and the rare visits of friends had been made when he was lying helpless in a semi-dark room. Thus nobody in the district had an exact impression of Sears' features. All his boyhood associates had died; I could find none who might be able positively to identify him. The arrival in Maryland had, of course, entirely changed the suspected man's environment of acquaintances; and, in short, there seemed no reason why William Sears should not drag out his existence indefinitely, or at least until he reached so patriarchal an age — a hundred twenty-five, for instance — that the long-suffering pension office would finally lose patience and cease the payment of his pension.

I was frank with the woman when I visited her upon her farm in Maryland, and she met me with apparent ingenuousness. More than that, she called her grandfather down, and the old man came hobbling briskly out upon the porch to welcome me. His rheumatism, he said, had been cured by a certain widely exploited medicine three years before, and the company had made a feature of his portrait in its advertisements. Certainly the pair now courted all possible publicity. With the early history of William Sears and with his war record, the old man showed an intimate knowledge — but then the woman might have posted him. Altogether, though I was convinced that the fellow was an impostor, I could not prove the government's case; and the more I was baffled the stronger became my determination. Hence my summoning of Peter Crewe.

We journeyed down to Bristow, the village nearest to the farm, and took up our residence in the local hotel. After a few days' caution we broke the ice, and the landlord did not have to be drawn out, either. He was full of indignation. A rascally government had sent an agent down there recently with the object of robbing their oldest pensioner of his reward for serving his country. Everybody for miles around knew and respected old Bill Sears. Last Decoration Day he had headed the procession of war veterans, in spite of his years, wearing his old blue uniform as proudly as though it had been a king's coronation robe. Bristow has been a Republican district, but, by heck, he knew a few who were going to vote Democrat at the next election to show the government what they thought of it.

'He's proud of his uniform, then?' asked Crewe.

'Proud of it, sir?' reiterated the landlord. 'Why, he won't go out of the house unless he's wearing it. Pretty soiled and stained and moth-eaten it is by now, too, but it represents his country in his eyes.'

'I remember he was wearing it when I visited the farm,' I said. 'It's almost gray by now, it's faded so much.'

'Anybody could get hold of an old Federal uniform,' said Crewe to me. 'That, of course, proves nothing, Langton. Very probably it's the same uniform that his predecessor wore in Kansas — assuming, of course, that there was a predecessor.'

'Look for the bullet wound under the hole in the coat,' said my companion.

This simple solution of the matter had actually never occurred to me. In my zeal to entrap the old fellow in some verbal inaccuracy I had neglected this most elementary method of testing at least part of his story.

On the following day, Crewe and I tackled him in the parlor. 'Now, Mr. Sears,' I said, 'with reference to that wound of yours, to remove all further doubt, will you lay bare the upper portion of your chest and let us see the scars?'

They flared up, the man and woman simultaneously. 'Don't let them strip you, Grandfather!' she cried, with an outburst of angry tears. 'These snippets of clerks have insulted you long enough. My grandfather fought and shed his blood for his country,' she continued proudly, 'and he's not going to be examined at his age as though he were a horse.'

'In that case, madam,' I answered, 'I shall be compelled to advise the government to stop payment of the pension money.'

'Very well, strip me!' the old man shouted. 'I'm not ashamed of any honorable scar. Go away, child. Let them look at the marks the bullets made; they're more than *they've* got to show.'

He removed his collar and laid bare the upper portion of his chest; and there, directly beneath the patch in the coat, was an undeniable scar! Then, while Crewe and I looked at each other in astonishment, he resumed his clothing with an air of triumph, leaving us baffled.

'Well,' I said to Crewe later, 'that ends the case.'

'No,' said Crewe decisively, 'there's still one thing to do. I have positive proof, Langton, that the man lied to us. That uniform, faded as it may be, never saw

Chancellorsville. Now we must bring such pressure to bear on them that they'll voluntarily give up the fight. We must meet fraud with fraud; it is the only way.'

'How?' I asked.

'By bringing some false witness who'll claim to have been a war comrade of the alleged Sears. Have you any man old enough in the Pension Department who would have sense enough to play such a role correctly?'

I thought a moment, and then I remembered just such a man. He had been requisitioned in similar cases.

'There's old Turpin, the porter,' I answered. 'He actually served during the war and could play the part to perfection.'

'Good. Now let's bring him to the farm as an alleged acquaintance of Sears. Let him come in the pretended expectation of greeting his onetime comrade in arms. Let him meet this old impostor with astonishment and angrily denounce him. Do you think Turpin could play his part so convincingly that he'll deceive this man into believing that his trick has been discovered?'

'He can if anyone can,' I answered. Turpin was a practical joker whose propensity for mischief had more than once involved him in serious difficulties with the departmental heads. He was an Irishman with the dry humor of the Scot; a privileged character in his own humble sphere, and known to all as a brave soldier of the republic.

I wired my chief to send Turpin to us immediately. We met him at the station and at once began to coach him in the part he was to play.

'Remember, Turpin,' I said, 'you were an intimate friend of Sears during the war. You shared the same blanket with him during many a night. You've just heard of him, after believing him to be dead for twenty years or more. Now, understand, when you meet the alleged Sears, you'll fail to recognize him. Then, when he begins to talk about old times, you'll pretend to be convinced, lure him into garrulousness, and suddenly entrap him with some simple question — the color of a horse, a captain's name, or something that he couldn't possibly fail to remember.'

Turpin passed his hand across his

wrinkled forehead in a reflective manner. 'Suppose he agrees with me,' he said. 'Suppose I can't get him to contradict himself? Or suppose he says he forgot? You can't expect too much of a man who claims to be a hundred and four.'

'Then,' I said, 'you have him. If he agrees with what isn't true, he must be lying; if he disputes you, denounce him as an impostor.'

'I'm on now,' Turpin answered.

When we reached the farm, Mrs. Bolton welcomed us with her usual suavity. 'I know what you've come for, Mr. Turpin,' she said when we had introduced him. 'You want to trap Grandfather into confession that he wasn't in the war. It's only natural that the government should lose patience with an old soldier who's shed his life blood for his country when he gets to be a hundred and four.'

'Not at all, ma'am,' said Turpin hotly. 'The government honors its old army men.' And I could see that the woman's subtle suggestion was working in him, and that we could not wholly reckon upon his sympathies.

However, when we met the veteran in the parlor, Turpin played his part to perfection. He darted forward and wrung him by the hand. 'Bill Sears!' he shouted. 'By gum, but you've changed, comrade. I'll wager you remember me though — Johnny Turpin.'

Sears looked at him closely. 'I don't seem to remember you,' he said. 'But I'll take your word, comrade. Sit down and smoke. It ain't as good as that home-cured plug we smoked before Richmond, when the commissariat give out — you remember that?'

'No,' said Turpin, 'I don't. The best of my remembrance is that the government had more tobacco than we *could* smoke. If my memory don't fail me we captured a tobacco convoy, going to Charleston.'

They looked at one another for a few moments, each sizing the other up. Then Sears spoke with a cutting inflection. 'Maybe you was a mule-whacker, comrade,' he said. 'Them fellers used to get all the food and tobacco while we poor ordinary soldiers went hungry.'

'*Mule-whacker?*' shouted Turpin indignantly. 'My belief is that you wasn't in the war at all. Bill Sears was as like you as a hog's like a prairie hen. Say, comrade, who was that little fellow that jumped into our redoubt at Gettysburg, and what did we do to him?'

'I wasn't at Gettysburg,' said the old man angrily. 'And it's my belief that you wasn't neither. Our company — Company B — was bridge-guarding at that time. How did you happen to get to Gettysburg if you was in Company B?'

Turpin was obviously disconcerted. The alleged Sears had him at a disadvantage, and he was aware of it. 'You was at Gettysburg, was you?' continued Sears in sneering accents. 'It's my belief Bull Run was the nearest you ever got to Gettysburg. You was a three-months' soldier, wasn't you?' He continued in this strain, Turpin sitting rigid and white under the abuse and invective that poured from the old fellow's lips. Suddenly Turpin leaned forward eagerly; his tension relaxed and a smile began to play about his features.

'You're right, comrade,' he said. 'I guess I have been lying to you. But it was lies in a good cause, to save the Grand Army from being imposed on by rascals. I wasn't in your company at all. I never knew Bill Sears. But I know you. Do you want to know why I wasn't at Gettysburg?' He leaned forward and hissed into the old man's ear. 'Because I had been drawn to flog a deserter.'

The old man seemed to crumple up. He sank back into his chair and stared wildly around him; at Peter Crewe, at me, at the implacable Turpin.

'Gentlemen,' said Turpin, turning to us, 'you brought me here to trap this fellow into lying. I couldn't do it. But it was a fortunate thing you did, for I guess I'm the only living man that can identify him for what he is. The morning before Gettysburg, while our boys was moving forward to meet the Rebs, I was kept behind in camp to flog a deserter. That was the man, and I strung him up to the triangle and laid the stripes on hard for the sake of the republic. Our uniforms was mostly worn out and we was fighting in anything we could find to put on our backs — and this fellow, he'd only joined three weeks before and hadn't got into the blue. That was the only thing that saved him from facing a firing squad. I laid the stripes on hard, and if you'll look at his back, you'll find them there to this day, gentlemen.'

Then I understood why the impostor had at first refused to let us strip him. And if we had only looked!

Turpin stood up, towering over the little shrunken old man who crouched in the chair. Once more he seemed about to carry out the sentence, and his adversary to cower in anticipation of it.

Suddenly the door opened and Mrs. Bolton glided in. She had evidently heard the whole of the colloquy, for she stood facing us all defiantly.

'The game's up, Annie,' said the old fellow in a weazened voice. The weight of his years appeared to have fallen about him, as though nothing but the will to live and the desire of perpetuating his imposture had hitherto braced up his failing powers.

I stepped forward. 'You had better confess the whole matter,' I said. 'It's possible that the government won't care to prosecute. In fact, I think I can promise you that this will be the case. Where *is* William Sears?'

'Dead,' said the woman sullenly. 'He died in Kansas, and we buried him in his blue uniform. It was the only thing he saved when our house burned down.'

'And who is this man?'

'Our hired man in Kansas. He looked like Grandfather, only younger. Grandfather often used to say, laughingly, 'When I'm dead, Annie, you can pretend Mulligan's — '

'Mulligan!' cried Turpin. 'That's the name, Mulligan!'

''You can pretend Mulligan's me and let him draw my pension.' I took it as a joke at the time, but it was no joke when the pension stopped, with all we had burned up with our home.'

'And he impersonated your grandfather?'

The woman nodded.

'And the bullet scar under the uniform?'

'A vaccination scar,' the woman answered.

Then Crewe took up the conversation. 'When you decided to have this man impersonate your grandfather,' he said, 'you wondered where you could obtain a Grand Army uniform. You knew that, though you might obtain one, the story might leak out. You couldn't afford to take any chances. And so you bought a length of cloth the color of the faded uniform, and you tore it and patched it and let it bleach for weeks in the sun. And then you made a uniform to fit this — Mulligan.'

'How'd you know that?' the woman cried, turning on Crewe swiftly. 'It's true — my God, it's true — but how did you *know* it?'

'If this Mulligan had ever worn the uniform, he would have been too wise to let you do what you did. If *any* man who ever saw him wearing it had used his eyes, he would have detected the imposture. Madam, you sewed the buttons on the *wrong side of the coat*. It's only women's clothes that button from right to left. Men's clothes button from left to right.'

10

The Face of the Clock

Readers of these memoirs have often said to me: 'Why do you lay so much stress upon Peter Crewe's optical powers, when the solution of many of these cases was due quite as much to the fertility of his mind and his deductive powers, as to his ability to remember everybody and everything that he had ever seen?'

My answer to this criticism has been that, while Crewe possessed in a marked degree the ordinary detective instinct, yet in almost every case it was his optical gift that started him along the correct line of investigation. It was his power of calling up an exact scene, a footprint on a carpet, a misspelled letter in a manuscript, the slightest deviation from the normal, which no one else could have discovered, that furnished him with his clues.

Take, for example, the case of the

murder of Walter Bentley. Everybody suspected, or at least sensed, the fact that he had been killed by Sewell. But it was Crewe who, by means of this power of his, afforded us proof positive of Sewell's guilt. Once the pistol trap had been laid bare, Sewell was shown to have purchased the weapon, he was identified by a dozen persons, a net of circumstantial evidence was woven around him independently of the confession which he afterward retracted, and ultimately he paid the penalty for his crime.

Bentley had moved into his palatial apartments a month after Sewell vacated them. He had rented them ready-furnished; and thus, before he left, Sewell was enabled to lay his trap. Had Bentley known who the last occupant had been, he would never have taken up his abode there; but Sewell had engineered the matter cunningly, having first lived there under an alias, and subsequently secured Bentley's tenancy through a series of adroit matters. He had worked the scheme with such perfection that he got Bentley as his successor. That was all he wanted.

If ever a man had cause to hate another, Sewell had cause to hate Bentley. The man had ruined him by underselling his Once-a-Year Clock, in whose patent a flaw existed, and flooding the market with an inferior product. Then he had foreclosed a mortgage, left Sewell penniless, and finally alienated his wife's affections. Sewell had pondered over these things until he became indubitably insane. He should have been sent to an asylum; but he was found guilty of murder, for the jury considered that no lunatic could have contrived so ingenious a conspiracy.

Bentley was highly pleased with his new apartment, which he considered a bargain. So it was; that was part of the lure. When he saw one of his own brand of Once-A-Year Clocks ticking merrily upon the mantel, he laughed and rubbed his hands, thinking how he had ousted Sewell, the inventor. Altogether, Bentley was in a high good humor.

Gordonia Mansions, where Bentley lived, was in one of those parts of the city in which the past and the future seem to be struggling for supremacy. It was an old house, and the district had once been fashionable. When Bentley was found dead upon the floor of his dining room, an ugly bullet wound in his head and a hole in the plaster of the wall, it was decided that a stray shot from the tenements across the street must have caused his death. Suspicion was for a time drawn toward Sewell, who had been breathing out threats of murder; but Sewell had been staying in a country house 20 miles from Gordonia Mansions, and had been there a week at the time of Bentley's death. The coroner's jury brought in a verdict of 'found dead,' and the matter dropped out of public notice.

It was Mrs. Bentley who urged me to investigate the affair. She had obtained her divorce from Sewell, had married Bentley, and, knowing the ruthless and relentless character of her former husband, besides being crazed with grief over Bentley's death, resolved to bring the murderer to justice. Although I had little faith in her suspicions of Sewell, I enlisted Peter Crewe's aid in the matter.

The apartment had been left just as it

was at the time of Bentley's death. Crewe and I went there to investigate. Dust lay thickly over everything; the bullet hole remained in the wall. Crewe took his station in the doorway and let his eyes travel slowly around the room. In those long glances he was photographing upon the sensitive retina of either eye the exact presentiment of everything within the boundary of those four walls. Never thenceforward, I knew, would the smallest particular be forgotten by him.

'The bullet came through this wall from the outside,' said Crewe, indicating the bullet hole, 'and went clear through Bentley's skull. Where did it go then? It wasn't found?'

'No. That was commented on at the inquest. The apartment was searched thoroughly, but it had disappeared. The theory advanced was that, its force spent, it changed its course, passed through the open door leading into the kitchen, and dropped through the open window looking upon the next street.'

'*If* the door was open,' said Crewe. 'But . . . ' He strode through into the kitchen, calling for me to follow him. 'That kitchen window isn't in a straight line with the open door. The bullet must have gone round a corner.'

'Well, where do you suppose it went?' I asked.

Crewe did not reply, but walked over to the clock and stood regarding it meditatively. It was a heavy ornamental piece of manufacture, wound once a year in accordance with the pirated principle of Sewell's clocks, and it ticked slowly and somberly, as though it were the sole guardian of the mystery.

'Do you see anything peculiar about this clock?' asked Crewe, looking at me amusedly. 'It's hardly possible that you don't.'

'No, I don't,' I said. 'Of course the principle is different; the ornamentation — '

'Tut! Look at the face.'

'It seems a very ordinary face,' I said.

'How many clocks have you looked at in your life, Langton? A dozen? A thousand?'

'More likely a thousand,' I said.

'And you *really* never saw a clock whose face appeared radically different from *that* one?'

'Not that I can recall,' I said, looking at the clock hopelessly.

'Well, it seems incredible,' said Crewe. 'Now, Langton, come to the window and direct your gaze upon the clock in the church spire. You see it clearly?'

'I can make out the figures and the hands.'

'Now look back. You see no difference?' He unfastened the glass front and, striking a match, held it to the central aperture in the face, through which the mechanism was wound. Not satisfied by this scrutiny, apparently, he drew a tiny battery from his breast pocket, connected two wires and pressed a knob, whereupon a little light flashed in a miniature bulb. He inserted this in the aperture and looked into the clock. Next, having closed the case again, he strode back across the room until he stood halfway between the mantel and the hole in the wall, upon a carpet still disfigured with Bentley's life-blood, which had made a dark stain there. He bent down and, with his pocket knife, cut a hole in the carpet. Underneath I saw the wiring of electrical connections. Crewe rose once more, crossed to the mantel and looked at the baize-coated wires that ran down the side of the mantel from the roof to floor.

'You see this?' he asked, indicating a branch which led into the clock.

'Yes. What purpose does it serve?'

'Primarily,' said Crewe, 'it connects the clock telegraphically with the official chronometer of the astronomical department. That, as you probably have read in the advertisements, was a special feature of the Once-a-Year Clock, both Sewell's and Bentley's, which in consequence was guaranteed to keep accurate time for the whole period of the twelve months. Actually, it served the purpose of the murderer. Now, Langton, I see that you begin to suspect the secret, and if you can tell me how that clock differs from that clock in the church tower, I'll explain the mystery.'

'Why does it differ?' I demanded rather angrily.

'There,' said Crewe, smiling, 'you have me. That will be for the murderer to explain. But if it didn't differ, I should never have hit upon the discovery. And now for Sewell. Where is he?'

'In town,' I answered. 'He says he's cooperating with the police in tracing the murderer.'

'Where is he living?'

'At his club — the National, according to this morning's papers.'

'I didn't read them. Does it say anything more about his lawsuit against the Bentley Company?'

'Yes,' I said, suddenly remembering. 'He's settled the case. He places the full rights of the patent at their disposal, upon condition that the Bentley people call in as many of their clocks as they can purchase and make them on his superior model. There's also a small cash settlement.'

'But why does he wish all the Bentley clocks called in?'

'Because he wants the honor of the invention; he wants it as he invented it, and the Bentley people are willing enough to replace the few hundred they've disposed of — '

So lame did Sewell's reason seem to me that I advanced it hesitatingly, as though it were some pitiful personal excuse. But before Crewe could answer, there came a tap at the door. The janitor stood there.

'Pardon me, gentlemen,' he said, 'but Mr. Sewell has sent for the clock.'

'What clock? This?' said Crewe. 'What right has Mr. Sewell to it?'

'I mean Mr. Sewell, the manager for the Bentley people,' said the janitor. 'It's part of the apartments, gentlemen — goes with them, and the landlord's going to exchange it for a new one.'

'Can you tell the man to come back this afternoon?' asked Crewe, pressing a silver piece into his hand.

'All right, sir. Thank you,' said the janitor, withdrawing. 'Sorry to have disturbed you, gentlemen.'

'Now, Langton,' said Crewe, 'hurry round to police headquarters and get a couple of detectives here. Get the authority to seal the door. And have Sewell with you.'

I hurried away and made my request to the head of the city police. He was disposed to scoff at my demand; but he had a wholesome respect for Crewe, who had assisted him and incidentally made a fool of him on more than one occasion. He agreed to send round the two men at once. 'But as for Sewell,' he said, 'he's said to be at the National Club, but I can't guarantee it. There ain't no more suspicion attaching itself to him, and he comes or goes as he pleases. Still, I'll send Sergeant Connolly to ask him to meet some gentlemen at the Gordonia, if he can find him.'

A plan occurred to me. 'This matter is one that throws grave doubts upon Sewell's innocence,' I said, leaning over the chief of police as impressively as I could. 'We must make sure of him. We must have a warrant ready for service. Where's the nearest magistrate?'

'There's Mr. Randall; he'll issue one, if you can swear to sufficient facts,' he said. 'What *are* the facts?' he added, looking at me keenly. And then I remembered that I knew none. For how could I say 'because the clock in the apartment has a different face from the clock in the church tower, I believe Sewell to be a murderer?'

'Now I tell *you* what *I'll* do,' said the

chief of police, springing to his feet. 'I'll get Mr. Sewell myself.' He touched a bell and a boy entered. 'Tell Briggs to telephone Mr. Sewell, 48562 Old,' he said. 'Ask him if he would mind stepping over on a little matter of business. And send Murphy and Ball to me.'

When the policemen came in, he bade them briefly report to Crewe at the Gordonia and place themselves at his disposal. If necessary, the apartment was to be sealed. The men saluted and went off, grinning. The police chief looked after them resentfully.

'That's what your friend Crewe's done for me,' he said bitterly. 'He's made me the laughing stock of my men. He's demoralized the discipline of the force. And by thunder, I'm going to give him a chance now to make a fool of himself. If he's discovered any evidence against Mr. Sewell, after I've spent weeks on the job without finding a particle, I'll . . . I'll step out and let him have my job,' he concluded.

The boy came in. 'Mr. Sewell will be here in half an hour,' he said.

'All right,' replied the police chief. 'Sit down, Mr. Langton,' he continued. 'You won't mind waiting? All right; then Mr. Sewell and me and you'll go there together.'

Sewell was four minutes ahead of time. I had never set eyes on him before. He was a burly man about forty years of age, and carried himself with a certain indescribable nerve and swagger which, to my mind, seemed but to accentuate a certain inward trepidation. Certainly, I thought, if he were the murderer of Bentley, if he had actually come back to brazen out the affair and to defy justice, he had monumental audacity.

'Ah, Mr. Sewell,' said the police chief cordially. 'I want you to meet Mr. Langton. Mr. Langton is acting for the — er, the widow,' he said, trying to be delicate. 'But quite in a professional way, you know. They've found something or other in the apartment and want your aid.'

I saw the light of suspicion grow in Sewell's eyes as he stared into my face. Then the lids dropped and the face became inscrutable. 'By all means,' he replied. He took out his watch. 'I have an engagement at five. I can give you a hasty half hour, if that will help. What is this discovery?' he asked, turning on me abruptly. I saw a pulse begin to thump in his temple, and in that moment knew that the man before me was afraid, horribly afraid.

'I can't say,' I answered. 'It isn't mine. Mr. Crewe has something to ask.'

'An amateur detective,' explained the chief of police, in allusion to my friend.

'One of these would-be Arsene Lupins, eh?' said Sewell mockingly. 'All right, gentlemen. Do you want to put on the handcuffs?' He stretched out his hands playfully, while the pulse thumped furiously.

'I guess we can dispense with them,' answered the police chief easily. 'I'm sorry to bother you so much, Mr. Sewell,' he added apologetically. 'I think this time will be the last.'

'Well, I hope so,' said Sewell. 'Otherwise I shall move into the next block and baffle your detective department.'

We put on our hats and went into the street. A short walk brought us to the

Gordonia, where we found Crewe and the detectives waiting for us. Crewe motioned to us three to be seated. He did not take Sewell's hand, but looked at him with a half-smile that set the man's pulse beating again. In that brief moment I knew that Crewe had photographed Sewell's face upon his mind forever.

One thing I noted in particular: wherever else Sewell's roving glances fell, he never looked at the clock.

'I understand you've accepted the office of general manager for the Bentley Company, Mr. Sewell,' said Crewe.

'I have. What of it?'

Crewe did not reply, but drummed his fingers on his knees.

'And I understand you've made some new discoveries in this case,' said Sewell. 'May I ask what they are?'

'We've found several things,' Crewe answered. 'For instance, we know that the bullet, instead of passing from without inward, passed from within outward. Therefore, the mystery of the missing bullet is made clear. It went through that hole in the wall after it had passed through Mr.

Bentley's brain, not previously.'

I saw the police chief smile and whisper into Sewell's ear. The two detectives sat stolidly upon their chairs.

'That's very interesting,' said Sewell, rising, 'and may or may not be true. But I understand you invited me here for a purpose. Have you any further questions to ask of me?' He snapped his watch ostentatiously, as though he grudged each moment spent in the presence of us amateurs.

Crewe remained silent for a moment, more through abstraction than insolence. 'Only one, sir,' he answered finally.

'And what's that?' asked Sewell, sneering.

Crewe rose and placed himself between our guest and the door. He peered into his face. 'Why did you change the front of the clock?' he demanded indolently.

The effect of this question was amazing. All the insolence went out of Sewell's face. He sank back into his chair and pressed his hand over his heart. A bluish pallor spread over his features. He could not reply.

'Come, Sewell,' said Crewe more kindly. 'Tell us the story of how you killed Mr. Bentley.'

But Sewell's face remained of the same pallor, and he stared up into his inquisitor's countenance, his mouth partly open, his eyes glassy and fixed. He tried to reply, but instead sighed and rolled out of his chair upon the floor.

It was half an hour before we could revive him. The strain and tension of the past month were producing the reaction at last. While we opened his collar and dashed water into his face, Crewe went to the mantel and deftly removed the face of the clock. Inside, cunningly fixed and compressed among the mechanism, was a tiny gripless pistol whose muzzle of .22 caliber was in exact alignment with the winding aperture. Sewell's eyes lit upon this when he became conscious.

Crewe went over to him and read a brief confession of murder. Putting forth his hand feebly, Sewell signed his name. Then we summoned an ambulance and the two detectives escorted him to the nearest hospital, from which, in course of time, he was taken to court to stand his trial; and, as I have related, found guilty. I will not dwell upon the details of the punishment; suffice it to say that the sentence of the law was duly carried into effect.

It was shown at the trial with what amazing ingenuity Sewell had worked. How, having decided that Bentley was to die by the very instrument which he had stolen from him, he baited a trap that could not fail. Sewell had had an electrician's training, and it was an easy matter to connect the pistol in the clock, and to connect it with a certain spot on the floor in such a way that the pressure of a foot would complete the circuit and discharge the weapon. But he had done more. That nothing untoward might mar the success of his scheme, he had somehow become possessed of Bentley's exact height and had carried out a long series of experiments until he could be sure that the line of the bullet's path would cleave the center of Bentley's skull. And only when standing in a certain exact spot would Bentley complete the circuit. He must have crossed and re-crossed the floor a hundred times before his foot found the terminal; he might have lived weeks, months, even a year — but, sooner or later, coincidence would bring about that pressure of his foot upon the terminal, and Bentley's consequent destruction.

As to the face which Sewell had put on the clock: in removing the front, he had dropped and fractured the piece of porcelain which bore the lettering of the numerals. He had not dared purchase another clock, and since the parts of the clocks of the two rival companies were identical, he had gone to his own factory by night, after it had been forced to close, and, setting up the printing dies, had printed a new front, which he afterward brought back to the Gordonia and exchanged for the broken portion.

'How did you know that, Crewe?' I asked. 'What was the difference between the front that Sewell printed and that of a normal clock — of the church tower, for instance?'

'It was a singular event,' Crewe

answered indirectly, 'and seems to show that Providence, or rather *Nemesis*, follows closely upon the criminal. Sewell must have seen hundreds of clock fronts printed; and yet at the supreme moment, the habit of years deserted him, and he became as helpless as a novice. Langton, take out your watch. You have the Roman numerals. Look at the fourth hour. How is it printed?'

'Four strokes,' I said.

'Four *single* strokes,' said Crewe. 'A deviation from the Roman lettering. How would you write the Roman 'four' in manuscript?'

'An *I* and a *V*,' I cried with sudden enlightenment.

'That is *precisely* how Sewell printed the face of the Once-a-Year,' said Crewe.

11

The Broken Heel

One of the last cases which Peter Crewe solved during our final residences in England was that which I have called 'The Broken Heel.' The murderer almost escaped detection through the fallibility of the local police, who framed a theory which exactly fitted in with his desires; and, having formed it, with characteristic obstinacy they stuck to it until it became untenable by reason of the confession of the murderer himself.

Sir George Taunton had been a client of mine, having extensive interests in America, and it was partly to advise with him concerning these that I had joined Crewe in London. The news of Sir George's death shocked me greatly, for only the week previously we had lunched together at his London club, where he appeared to be the picture of health and destined for a ripe old age. When, therefore, I read of his murder in the newspapers, I immediately telephoned Crewe and met him at the railway station, from which we rode down to Little Whittlefield together.

Sir George Taunton had been a retired Egyptian official. For nearly twenty years he had given up brain and body to the government of Egypt; and with character- istic ingratitude, the Egyptian agitators had selected him as the butt of their ridicule and vituperation. At the height of recent agitations in Egypt, threats of murder, which had been made in the native press, had penetrated to Little Whittlefield. For some reason Sir George was more hated in seclusion than he had ever been in the activities of his official career, and his death was looked upon as the one thing necessary to gratify the longing for English blood which seemed to possess a portion of the native press.

The Taunton estate was situated in a lonely and remote part of the West Country. The high road led past it from the nearest town, Quantock, 11 miles away. On the other side of the Queen Anne mansion was a deep lake, about a mile in width, and covered with snow, beneath which lay, at this time, a good six inches of ice — for the winter had been exceptionally severe. Where the high road was fronted by the great gates stood the lodge of Evans, the porter. He was a man who had been for some years in Sir George's service and, although addicted to liquor, was considered trustworthy. It was Evans, together with Fisher, the local police inspector, who met us at the station and told us the facts concerning the tragedy.

On the morning of the previous day, Sir George's servants had found him lying dead in his bed, a knife in his heart. Upon his breast was a clipping from a newspaper, detailing briefly the threats that had been made against the ex-official by numerous Egyptian officials. Furthermore, a stranger — a South European, as had at first been thought, but, in the light of later facts, obviously an Egyptian — had been seen during the preceding week in Quantock, although he had subsequently disappeared. There was no doubt, said Fisher, that this man, having scaled the park wall, had entered Sir George's bedchamber and murdered him, afterward looting the house and escaping. No trace of him had yet been found.

'Then robbery was his object?' asked Crewe.

'We think it was an afterthought,' said Evans. 'Or perhaps he may have decided to add robbery to the other crime after entering the estate. He removed all the silverware, a quantity of the late Lady Taunton's jewels, which Sir George kept in a safe, and — '

'How did you know that they were in the safe?' asked Crewe, turning his gaze full upon Evans.

The porter flushed. 'The safe was in the bedroom,' he said defiantly. 'It was easy to suspect there were jewels inside.'

'And the peculiar thing,' said Fisher, the police inspector, 'is that he took the things away in a wheelbarrow.'

'A wheelbarrow?' said Crewe, musing. 'Well, we must examine the premises.'

'That won't do you any good, gentlemen,' said Fisher. 'The man is dead, and his barrow is with his body.'

'Dead?' queried Crewe.

'No doubt about it, though we're bound to make investigations on the off chance. Come with me, gentlemen, and I'll show you just how he entered and how he died.'

Fisher led us to the side entrance. All around the house were the tracks of the barrow — a single line, cut by the front wheel in the snow.

'Has it snowed since the murder?' Crewe demanded.

'Not a particle.'

'Then,' said Crewe emphatically, 'if these are wheelbarrow tracks, where are his boot prints?'

'That puzzled us for a long time, sir,' said Fisher. 'Finally we decided that he must have sat in the barrow and let it slide down this incline. You see the ground slopes considerable.'

'Then there would be marks of the barrow legs. How could he slide in it and hold it up at the same time?'

'He must have balanced himself before he started,' Fisher replied. 'And you see,

Mr. Crewe, every few yards the tracks cease and begin again a yard or more on one side. That's where the legs fell down and he covered up the tracks with snow. There was a slight thaw yesterday, and that hid the traces of his work.'

Crewe grunted but said nothing. Fisher led us round the house. The track of the wheel ran down to the frozen surface of the pond and thence across the ice in a series of curves interrupted every few yards and recommencing a little distance away. In the middle of the pond I saw a gap of black water. The wheel tracks ceased here; there were imprints of feet, but confused and irregular; then across the water, the barrow tracks began again and led to the opposite shore.

One thing I noticed. Across the water there was nothing but the single wheel track; but on the side nearer the mansion there were soft, shapeless holes in the snow at intervals of a yard or more on either side of the wheel markings.

'That's where the barrow legs went down,' said Evans, when Crewe pointed these out to him.

'Now, gentlemen, this is the theory of the police,' said Fisher. 'The murderer scaled the wall of the estate, which runs along the back of the other shore of the pond, and got into the pheasant woods, in which his barrow had been concealed. He wheeled it over the ice toward the mansion with the idea of using it for carrying away the plunder, probably to some vehicle which he had in waiting at a safe distance. He wheeled the barrow up to the house, entered, committed the crime, and started out, with the plunder dumped into the barrow. But the ice, which had borne the barrow when it was empty, would not support its weight when it was full. In the middle of the pond it broke, and he was drowned.' Fisher looked round at us triumphantly, as one who has solved the greatest of all mysteries.

'How deep is the pond where the ice is broken?' I asked.

'Fifty feet,' said Evans. 'Some say more.'

'Have you grappled for the plunderer, to make sure he or the loot is there?' I asked Fisher.

'Evans let down a line,' he said, 'but he couldn't find anything. The current is too swift; it would carry everything beneath the ice. We shall have to wait till spring.'

Meanwhile Crewe, apparently not noticing Fisher's explanations, was searching among the footprints round the hole. Presently he stooped down and picked up a small wet object which was floating on the surface of the water. It was the heel of a man's boot, but so abraded and water-soaked that it could not have been fitted with certainty to any shoe.

'Gentlemen,' said Crewe, raising himself, 'the search is at an end. You see that hole in the bank beside the lake?' He pointed to the entrance of a fox warren that appeared at the base of a knoll of sandy earth upon the opposite shore. 'You'll find everything there, I think.'

'Impossible!' cried Fisher, staring at him. I stared, too. Miraculous as had appeared to be some of Crewe's deductions, it seemed incredible that he could have solved this problem in so striking a fashion.

'If you're afraid that your fine theory will be shattered, of course you don't need to go there,' said Crewe, sneering at Fisher. And this attitude was so unusual a one with Crewe that I looked at him in greater astonishment than before.

'Well, sir,' said the porter Evans, who had been regarding Crewe attentively, 'if the gentleman says the stuff's there, and is so positive about it, at least there won't be no harm looking.'

'Right you are,' cried Fisher. 'I'll bet you five pounds, Mr. Crewe, that it's *not* there.'

'I never bet upon a certainty,' replied Crewe superciliously.

'Then let's go there at once and see!' hollered Inspector Fisher, stung by the taunt.

'What'd be the sense in his hiding the stuff down there?' asked the porter.

'Suppose you crawl in and bring it out for us, my man,' said Crewe, turning upon him.

'That I will, sir, for sure,' said Evans briskly. Accordingly, we started off toward the bank and, upon arriving there, Evans went down upon his hands and knees and thrust his head and arms into the hole, while Crewe stood immediately over him.

Presently Evans came out, very dirty, but manifestly triumphant. 'It's a blind hole,' he said, shaking the loose sand from his sleeves. 'There ain't no silver there, sir. Would you like to try for yourself?' he continued sneeringly.

'Yes, suppose *you* bring us out the silver, Mr. Crewe,' said Fisher patronizingly. 'It's a certainty, you remember.'

But Crewe only stood by, hanging his head, apparently dejected and humiliated. 'No, I must have made a mistake,' he said.

'People generally do who jump to such rapid conclusions,' said the policeman. 'I don't think, sir, that any American amateurs can improve upon the methods of the English police. We're slow, but sure — a phrase you may have *heard* in your own country, sir,' he concluded, the picture of easy triumph.

'Well,' said Crewe, 'I suppose you'll give me one more chance? I should like to meet you gentlemen at the porter's gate this time tomorrow. All I ask is a little time to think of some new theory.'

'All the time you want, Mr. Crewe,'

chuckled Inspector Fisher. And he started away with the porter, leaving Crewe and myself together. As they went, I could see their backs heaving with laughter. Evidently they were enjoying Crewe's discomfiture.

'Did you really think the silver was hidden in that hole?' I asked Crewe as we walked back toward the mansion where the housekeeper had fitted up a room for us.

'No,' he replied with a chuckle. 'I wanted an opportunity to inspect the soles of Evans' boots.'

'To see if the heel fitted?' I gaped.

'Not altogether. I was looking for the marks of what I hope to fish out of the hole tonight. Yet, as I suspected, he's had his boots re-heeled recently — probably did it himself, so there's nothing to be learned in that way.'

'What's in the hole?'

'The *real* wheelbarrow,' Crewe answered with a laugh. 'Will you be ready to come on a fishing trip with me when the moon gets up?'

'Of course,' I answered.

'I'll have secured a length of cord in the

nearby town,' said Crewe. 'Thirty feet will be ample. Evans was lying about the depth of the lake; one can see that from the configuration of the surrounding ground. And I have a grappling iron, or rather the hook of a letter file I took the liberty of securing from inside the window of Sir George's library while we were perambulating round the house. With these I think we shall discover what we want.'

'Crewe,' I hazarded, 'suppose you admit a variation upon your usual procedure.'

'In what way?'

'Up to now, you've told me what your clue was *after* the detection of the murder. Suppose this time you tell me in advance, so as to afford me the pleasure of working with you?'

'Well,' said Crewe, smiling, 'I will. The murderer is Evans, the porter, who entered his master's house upon a mission of robbery. He'd unlocked the safe, whose number he'd secured, when he turned to find Sir George wide awake and looking at him. He stabbed him to the heart with the bradawl he held in his hand.'

'How do you know it was a bradawl?'

'Because a bradawl was used in heeling his shoes, as I discovered when he was kneeling in front of that hole in the bank. To continue, after having perpetrated the murder, he was filled with consternation. Hastily slinging his booty, which was in a bag — '

'There was no barrow?'

Crewe shook his head. ' — over his back, he hurried away and concealed it — *where*? It's useless to inquire. We might search the estate for days without discovering this; and, after all, it's irrelevant to our purpose. Then, and then only, he remembered that he'd read in his Sunday newspaper of the threats made against his Sir George's life. That seemed to offer salvation. He stole back to the house and placed upon the dead man's breast the clipping from the newspaper, detailing these threats. Then he rushed off to Fisher and concocted some story — and the imagination of the towns-people furnished the dark stranger who had been lurking in the neighborhood, a lay figure who frequently appears after a mysterious murder.'

'How do you *know* all this?'

'I sensed it first,' said Crewe. 'Then I soon built up my criminal by the *heel*. To begin with, it was, though water-soaked, unusually small for a man's heel. A small heel means a small and rather narrow shoe. A shoe of that description means a light but not necessarily short man. The foot, of course, develops strictly in accordance with the body's need of support.

'I knew that the owner wasn't short because of the space between the foot tracks, indicating length of limb. Consequently, the owner of the heel was tall and slight. There are only three types of men in the world, Langton; the tall and slight, the short and slight, and the heavy man — whether tall or not is immaterial. Now, our friend Evans exactly answered the description which the heel afforded me.'

'But you could never convict a man upon such theorizing.'

'No. Of course, I merely used the theory as groundwork from which to build up facts. I got those when he was kneeling in front of the hole.'

'What were they?'

But Crewe became suddenly taciturn. 'Wait till we bring home the catch tonight,' he answered. 'Langton, I smell supper, and this country air has made me uncommonly hungry.'

The hours after supper seemed to spin out interminably. We smoked our pipes in the library until midnight, when a yellow arc on the eastern horizon indicated the rising of the moon. When it had mounted high enough to flood the country with its silvery light, Crewe and I set out silently from the house toward the lake, he carrying the file hook, I the length of cord. We reached the ice and, having reached the hole, which was already covered with a new coating, tied the hook to the cord, weighted it with a paperweight which Crewe took from his pocket, and let it descend. As Crewe had foretold, the 30 feet proved ample. We felt the weight strike the bottom when the cord was three-quarters out, and there ensued one of the most wearying explorations that I have ever known.

'Patience, always patience, Langton,' said Crewe to me. 'The chances are roughly about fifty to one against our striking what we want at each cast of the line. And then,' he added, as if in an afterthought, 'it may not be there. But it *must* be; there was nowhere else to throw it.'

That some object besides stones lay at the bottom of the pond was evident, for we felt the hook and the weight repeatedly strike against it; but every time the cord came up with nothing but the empty hook coated with slime. Again and again we grappled, though in vain. Once we brought the object of our search a yard or more from the bottom, but it fell back.

'Take a stroll and smoke, Langton,' said Crewe finally. 'This is one of the disagreeable tasks of a detective's life. We have six hours yet until daybreak.'

He took the cord from my numbed fingers and fished, patiently and persistently. I smoked one pipe . . . two . . . lit the third and thrust the stem into my tobacco-burned mouth. Suddenly I perceived that Crewe was hauling something out of the hole. He brought it to the level of the ice, and over. Then it dropped from the hook and fell clattering upon the

231

frozen surface with a metallic clang. I hurried toward the spot in time to see Crewe lift it in his hand with a low shout of joy. It was a slime-coated skate!

'Is that all?' I asked. 'Have we been fishing for that thing since midnight?'

'All?' Crewe repeated. 'Don't you know why I wanted it?'

'No.'

'There were marks of the clamp on the heel I found.'

'But you can't convict Evans — '

'And marks of the skate clamps on Evans's soles yesterday. But not on the heels.'

'You mean that Evans was wearing skates when he crossed the pond?'

'I mean,' said Crewe, rising, 'that the so-called wheelbarrow tracks were nothing but the tracks left by the skate-blades in the soft snow. That's why there were no footprints round the house, and not Fisher's absurd reason.'

'But there was only a single line.'

'Exactly. Did you ever hear of a skater going with both feet down? Were there not gaps in the lines? That was where

Evans shifted from one foot to the other. As I was saying this evening, Langton, I knew from the space between the lines that the wearer of the skates was tall. He came on skates because he knew what deadly witnesses boot prints are, although he didn't have sense enough to think of the wheelbarrow theory until Fisher so kindly obliged him. The marks across the ice were made the following night.'

'The following night?' I echoed.

'Precisely. When Fisher gave him his clue, Evans wasn't slow to take it. He skated to the opposite shore, then turned again. But in the middle of the pond he lost his skate. Langton,' said Crewe, turning to me, 'didn't you think of skates when you saw the floating heel? Is there anything but a skate that will pull a heel from a boot? His heel came off. Thereupon he broke a hole in the ice and flung the skate into the water.'

'Why not both?'

'He needed one skate on which to return. He might have carried the useless skate, but you must remember that his brain was in a whirl; and his guiding impulse, from first to last, was to get rid of evidence. So he returned on one skate, putting his foot down from time to time to prevent fall — or rather the toe of his boot. That formed the blunt holes in the snow which Fisher ascribed to the legs of the wheelbarrow.'

'Poor evidence on which to convict,' I said.

'Unless a confession can be forced,' Crewe answered. 'Remember, Langton, that we aren't dealing with a normal man. He's passed through agonies of fear during these days. Yesterday his triumph over me brought about an intense reaction. He's probably been drinking all night. He's in that condition of mind common to patients under the influence of chloroform: at a certain stage they will tell everything that's asked them. Now some sudden shock that will bring about another psychic revolution may act upon his mind with overwhelming force — '

He broke off and paced slowly back to the house, deep in thought. He did not even hear my questions.

Crewe had sent me ahead of him for

the meeting the following day. I had been chatting at the lodge with Fisher and Evans for some minutes after the appointed hour, and still Crewe did not make his appearance.

'I think,' said Fisher sarcastically, 'your friend, the amateur, has had enough detective experiences to last him for some time. I shouldn't be surprised if he failed to turn up at all.'

'He's a damn fool,' blurted out Evans, whose flushed face and trembling hands indicated that he had been celebrating his success rather too freely.

'Waiving that point,' said Fisher with a laugh, 'where *is* this celebrated detective friend of yours? My duty won't permit — '

He sprung round swiftly. I started. Evans jumped back and yelled as Crewe's hand fell on his shoulder from behind.

'I lost my skate in the hole in the ice,' he said. 'Evans,' he continued, seizing the porter by the arms and peering into his face, 'the game's up. Mr. Fisher, take him. What — ? Why, look at his face, man, look at his *face*!'

But Evans had fallen in the snow, and, kneeling there, he blurted out the story of his crime.

12

The Death in the Dirigible

'Simplicity, Langton, if I may use a metaphor, is the keystone of the arch of successful crime. We have the upward curve — the plot; the downward curve — its accomplishment. Unless the whole is bound with that simplicity of design which ensures success, the plot must fail.'

Most illustrative of this, I think, was Crewe's detection of the diabolical plan of the French doctor, which resulted in the death of four men and the destruction of two German government balloons.

The German government, there was no doubt, had at last perfected a dirigible balloon whose value as a war weapon was incalculable. Whether or not the French government was privy to the murderous acts of Dr. Fenelon cannot be known for certain. He may have been a self-inspired patriot. There is no doubt, however, that his intention was to intimidate the German government into abandoning this type of balloon, which had been constructed at the cost of so much labor and enterprise.

You all remember the fate of the Kaiserin II and her successor, the Kaiserin III; how each ended in a similar manner. Each, after remaining in the air for forty-eight hours or so, and after hovering immediately over the French defensive works upon the boundary, collapsed while at an altitude of perhaps eight hundred feet, dashing its two occupants to the ground and instantaneously killing them. The balloon, in both cases, remained only as a thing of shreds and patches of silk, and a tangle of wickerwork.

Crewe and I, who were both interested in aeronautics, had been present at the start of each balloon from Hamburg. There we made the acquaintance of Dr. Fenelon. Despite his French name and accent, he had ingratiated himself into the confidence of the German war staff as an inhabitant of Alsace-Lorraine — as one of those French-born citizens who had elected to throw in their fortunes with the

German nation after that province was wrested from Napoleon. He had been a child when the war ended; he was now a man of between forty and fifty years, a doctor in the new aeronautical division of the German army, and an avowed hater of France. His task was to attend the starting of the balloonists, to test their hearts and lungs before they ventured into the upper air; he had free access to the balloon, which was held captive within the military reservation. Crewe and I had permits to enter, for these were accorded freely to all with satisfactory references. The secret lay in the manufacture, and none could ascertain it from an external inspection of the great globe.

It was while the third balloon was preparing to start, after the destruction of the two others, that Crewe resolved to ascertain, if possible, the cause of the disasters.

'You're courageous,' he said to Lieutenant Von Kelter, 'to risk your life after your predecessors have perished.'

'It's part of my job,' Von Kelter answered, with a fatalistic shrug of his shoulders. 'If I die, well . . . '

'You don't believe in the rumors of foul play?' I asked.

'Impossible,' Von Kelter answered. 'However, this time I shall make the ascent unaccompanied, so that treachery will be impossible.'

'The balloon might be tampered with before you start.'

'Hardly. None but our officers can approach the tent in which it is moored. Then, before ascending, I shall test the pull-cord and all the apparatus.'

'And yet,' said Crewe, 'your compatriots were found dead in the shreds of their balloons — and they, too, had confidence. Now let me ask you a question. To what do you ascribe the fact that their bodies were found drenched with water?'

'Rain — or dew,' said the lieutenant.

'It hadn't rained, and dew could never have soaked their bodies to the skin and drenched their hair.'

'It's immaterial,' Von Kelter answered. 'I shall not die, for I've tested the balloon thoroughly and have complete confidence in it.'

This conversation took place upon the morning on which the ascent was to be made. Almost immediately afterward, the tent was stripped from the balloon, and the huge inflated sphere could be seen swaying above the ropes which fastened it to the earth. Sphere-shaped instead of cigar-shaped, the steering apparatus was hidden within; it looked like a balloon of an old-fashioned type, such as has been in use during the past hundred years. It rose by the aid of hydrogen gas; yet, in some mysterious way, the builder had made it completely responsive to its driver's hand.

Dr. Fenelon now came forward to make the physical examination. The process proved lengthy. Crewe, who by some process known to himself alone had obtained leave for us both to be present, watched the doctor intently.

'I doubt — I fear,' stammered the doctor, 'your condition doesn't wholly warrant your ascending. There's no organic derangement, but the heart contractions are a little feeble. At a high altitude . . . ' He broke off, hesitating. 'Have you ever inhaled oxygen, Herr Lieutenant?' he asked.

'Every chance I get,' he replied facetiously.

'No, I mean, via an air-tank.'

'Once, when I had pneumonia, to ease the lungs.'

'I would counsel you to let me place a small tank in the basket,' the doctor said. 'Then when at a height, if you find the rarity of the air oppressive, you can take a few breaths from the inhaler.'

'Very well,' said the lieutenant indifferently. The doctor summoned his assistant, and they placed a small tank in among the thermometers, hygrometers and other instruments for gauging the atmospheric conditions. And at that moment I saw Crewe's face light up and knew that he had solved the mystery, for I had seen that expression often, and it never failed to be productive.

The lieutenant climbed into the car, which rested a few feet above the level of the ground. All but one of the ropes were unfastened, and to that one a dozen soldiers clung with all their power, while the enormous gas-dilated sphere swayed like an intoxicated thing, striving to leap upward and gain the security of the skies. Meanwhile, Crewe had gone hastily toward the chief of the aeronautical staff, who was standing by, and conferred hurriedly with him. What he said, I do not know. His arguments must indeed have been cogent, and probably backed by some authority unknown to me; for just as the men were about to cast off the rope, I saw General von Stimm wave his hand toward the lieutenant and shout to him to descend.

The lieutenant climbed hastily out of the wickerwork basket. At the same time, somebody — Crewe, as I discovered afterward, but in the confusion he was unnoticed — shouted to the men to release the rope. Instantly the balloon shot up into the skies, leaving the lieutenant standing, mortified, upon the ground, watching its upward flight.

This contretemps sent the general into a furious passion. The balloon was as good as lost; its course had taken it out toward the North Sea with little hope of its recovery. He issued order to his adjutant and, a moment or two afterward, while I still stared round to discover my companion, I found myself under arrest. I was conveyed to the general's headquarters, along with Crewe, who had been apprehended in another section of the enclosure as he was trying to leave. Ten minutes later we were hauled into his presence.

'Who the devil are you?' he shouted roughly in guttural English. 'Unless you can offer a suitable explanation, you shall both be placed under arrest as spies. You have spoiled the Kaiserin IV — the devil take it, another balloon to go!' He gnashed his teeth in mortification.

At his side stood the lieutenant, his face pallid, his brow covered with sweat.

'General,' said Crewe quietly, 'when I was a younger man, I spent some months in Germany.'

'Well, what the devil has that to do with me?'

'May I speak to you privately?' asked Crewe. 'It concerns a beer garden, and a youthful officer whose sword was stolen.'

The general became paler than the lieutenant. 'Gentlemen, you may leave me,' he said; and, saluting, the lieutenant and the orderly departed.

'Now, General,' said Crewe briskly, 'if I alluded to an unfortunate incident in your early career, which I witnessed when you were a subaltern, it wasn't for the purpose of seeking immunity through my knowledge of it. It was necessary, in your own interest, that I should gain your ear. Indeed, I gave the order which resulted in the releasing of the balloon. If I hadn't done so, the lieutenant's life would have been sacrificed. As that balloon comes down to land, it will surely come down in fragments, and drenched with water.'

'Why?' asked the astonished general.

'Because you have a traitor upon the staff of your division, and his name is Fenelon. It is he who destroyed the two dirigibles that preceded this, and was the cause of the death of four officers.'

'Your proofs?' asked the general in a strained voice.

'They'll be found when the balloon comes to earth — an event which has probably occurred already, owing to atmospheric conditions, in which event it will be found before nightfall. Let me ask you a question. What were the contents of the last balloon that was sent up?'

'Identical with those of the first,' the general answered. 'A barometer, two thermometers, a hygrometer, field glasses, and certain military and motor equipment of a private nature.'

'And a tank of oxygen in case the balloonist suffered from the effects of the rarified air?'

'I believe so. What has *that* to do with it?'

'First, General, let me entreat you to place Dr. Fenelon under arrest immediately.'

The general struck a bell upon the table. Two orderlies came in. 'Take these men,' he said, 'and confine them in the guard house. Tomorrow they will be arraigned before a military court as spies.'

'You're *mad*, General!' cried Crewe angrily. 'I tried to save you — '

'You tried to *intimidate* me, sir,' shouted the general, 'and to exculpate yourselves by maligning the honor of a brave officer. Take them away immediately.'

We were hauled off ignominiously across

the officers' quarters in the direction of the guard house, while General von Stimm followed us to the door and stood upon the threshold, watching us sourly. As our captors led us across the quadrangle of green, I noticed a commotion in a further corner of the square; then an officer came hurrying along, bearing a newspaper in his hand. He passed us, and I read the staring headline:

'DESTRUCTION OF THE GREAT DIRIGIBLE.'

Crewe had seen it as well. He smiled grimly. 'If only they'd arrested Fenelon,' he muttered. 'Why, there he goes, Langton.'

Surely enough, the Alsatian doctor came strutting along the path, dressed in full regimentals. He saw us from afar and, fuming, came toward us, halting close at hand.

'Ha, the spies!' he said viciously. 'You will find it goes hard with you, for we do not love spies in Germany.'

'You're lying,' said Crewe; and, breaking from his captor, he struck the doctor upon his face with his open hand. Instantly the doctor drew his sword and rushed at the aggressor. Crewe seized the point of the blade the moment it left the scabbard and, with a powerful wrench, snapped it in two and threw the pieces to the ground. I saw blood follow them from his wounded hands.

As for the orderly, he stood as if petrified. From every quarter officers came running up. The doctor, overwhelmed by this disaster, which meant, according to the German code, dismissal from the service, remained with hanging head upon the gravel path.

'Doctor, you must consider yourself under arrest,' said the adjutant, coming up to him and taking him by the arm. 'As for these fellows . . . ' He looked as if he were about to run us through. His fingers twitched upon the hilt of his sword. Then he issued a brief command, and the orderlies seized us by the arms and forced us over the quadrangle into the guard house.

'It'll go hard with us unless you can prove your case, Crewe,' I said later.

'But I can,' he said confidently. 'I snapped

his sword, Langton, not only in self-defense, but so that he might be detained in the barracks. We mustn't let that murderer escape. If he could have resisted the temptation to taunt us, he would doubtless be on his way to the frontier, for he knew that he was discovered.' He went to the door. 'Orderly,' he called, 'I wish to send a note to the general.' He scribbled a few words on a sheet of paper and handed it to the man along with a gold piece. The orderly took both in silence and turned away.

'What did you write, Crewe?' I asked.

'Why, very little, Langton,' he answered. 'You've often been pleased to comment upon my faculty for remembering every face that I've ever seen during my lifetime. Now the fact is that, when I was in Germany many years ago, I saw General von Stimm four times — twice under discreditable circumstances. This is a little reminder, stronger than the last. It will bring him.'

It did. Half an hour later we were again in the general's presence. His face was white with agitation, and he wiped his damp brow nervously. 'How much do you want?' he asked Crewe bluntly.

'General,' said Crewe, 'once before you misunderstood my offer and, but for a lucky circumstance, a murderer would have continued to disgrace the German uniform. I want no money. I want to punish him and save the army's honor. The balloon has been found?'

'Yes,' he answered.

'It won't be touched or moved for twenty-four hours?'

'Not for two days. Soldiers are guarding the place where it fell.'

'It was destroyed?'

The general nodded.

'Take us there immediately. And let a military court be ready to convene the moment you return, for Dr. Fenelon will have to stand trial for murder.'

'When do you wish to start?'

'Within the hour,' Crewe answered.

'Gentlemen,' said the general, 'I do not know who the devil you are, or why you have come here, but it shall be as you request. You are freed from arrest. I will drive with you to the railroad station and thence accompany you to the locality.'

We arrived at a small village some eighty-five miles distant from Hamburg. A special train was requisitioned, and at eight o'clock that evening we three disembarked at the railroad station. It was not yet dark, and when we had crossed the main street in the direction of open country, we saw a large crowd gathered around the remnants of the balloon.

A quarter of a mile's walk brought us to the spot. A company of soldiers who were on guard admitted us to the site where the dirigible lay. It had fallen from an immense height, and with incredible velocity, for the wickerwork of the basket was smashed into innumerable chips of wood which lay strewn over the ground, while the speed of the descent had ripped the gas bag from its frame covering so that hardly a particle of it remained. Within a radius of a hundred yards lay the broken remnants of the instruments. But the most singular fact was that, while the surrounding land was parched from drought, the balloon's remnants rested in a pool of water some two feet deep, which had gathered into a depression on the ground; and water had drenched the wickerwork and the pieces of the instruments.

Crewe stooped and rummaged among these last. Presently he rose; in his hand he held a piece of twisted metal, nickel or aluminum. Upon one side was stamped OXYGEN. 'Do you recognize this, sir?' he asked the general.

'It is merely a portion of the tank of oxygen,' Von Stimm rejoined.

'Which would pass out through tubes, at the disposition of the aeronaut — isn't that so?'

'Certainly.'

'Now, if the metal weren't perfectly airtight, it's obvious that the gas would speedily leak out and dissipate itself in the atmosphere. Am I correct, General?'

'I believe that is correct. Obviously an oxygen tank must be entirely airtight.'

'Then see these,' said Crewe, holding up the fragments for Von Stimm's closer inspection. Along the edge of the metal were drilled innumerable tiny holes, such as a pin's point might have made. 'Quite large enough for a leakage. Especially today, when the sun's rays have been strongly actinic. In cloudy weather, when there was considerable vapor pressure in the atmosphere, it might have taken two days, as with the last balloons, before the explosion.'

'You mean, sir, that the oxygen was designed to escape? But suppose that were so — is oxygen inflammable?'

I was as perplexed as the general. Crewe placed the metal in his hands. 'That will be vital evidence,' he said. 'General, suppose that oxygen *does* leak into an atmosphere surcharged with escaping hydrogen? You know the hydrogen won't remain even in the silk bag more than a limited time. Now, bring oxygen and hydrogen together in the right proportion. Suppose the proportions have been carefully calculated, so that eventually they're obtained. Suppose we have the formula H_2O. That signifies — ?'

'Water.'

'Obviously. It was only necessary, therefore, for Fenelon to send up the balloon with the hydrogen gas bag and the oxygen tank, and to calculate the leakage from either so closely that eventually they would ignite. What happens? The gasses rush together with a thunderclap, combine into water, and the sphere falls to the ground, drenched in the fluid. General, with the help of this evidence we shall send Dr. Fenelon to the gallows.'

And so the sequel proved.

We do hope that you have enjoyed reading this large print book.

Did you know that all of our titles are available for purchase?

We publish a wide range of high quality large print books including:
Romances, Mysteries, Classics
General Fiction
Non Fiction and Westerns

Special interest titles available in large print are:
The Little Oxford Dictionary
Music Book, Song Book
Hymn Book, Service Book

Also available from us courtesy of Oxford University Press:
Young Readers' Dictionary
(large print edition)
Young Readers' Thesaurus
(large print edition)

For further information or a free brochure, please contact us at:
Ulverscroft Large Print Books Ltd.,
The Green, Bradgate Road, Anstey,
Leicester, LE7 7FU, England.
Tel: (00 44) **0116 236 4325**
Fax: (00 44) **0116 234 0205**

Other titles in the
Linford Mystery Library:

GIRL MEETS BOY

Jack Iams

Reunited with his English war bride, Sybil, after two years, Tim takes her back to the USA with him — but where to live, in the middle of the post-World War II housing crisis? They meet a friend of Sybil's deceased father, who promises to help. Next thing they know, the New Jersey chapter of the British-American War Brides Improvement Association arranges accommodation for them in the isolated coastal community of Merry Point. Here they meet their curmudgeonly landlord and an inept handyman. Then Sybil finds a body on the pier . . .

FIRE IN THE VALLEY

Catriona McCuaig

Spring is just around the corner in Llandyfan, and the first crocuses are beginning to bloom. Then the beautiful morning is shattered by the discovery of a corpse in the glebe — the victim of a grisly murder. Who could have wanted poor Fred Woolton, the mild-mannered milkman, dead? Midwife Maudie once again turns sleuth! Despite expecting a baby of her own, she is not about to take it easy while a case needs to be solved . . .

THE SHADOW

Donald Stuart

When Emma Mason inherits a house on Orkney from her Great-aunt Freda, she is mystified — she knows nothing about Freda, and her parents are of little help. The only thing for it is to visit Orkney herself. On the ferry, she meets Gregor McEwan, a wildlife photographer and passionate Orcadian. Together they begin to piece together Freda's story, whilst becoming increasingly attracted to each other — though there are serious obstacles in their way: Gregor is struggling with a past tragedy, and Emma's life is firmly rooted in Tyneside . . .